Five years was a long time, but she still *knew* him.

And if the Jack Alcott she knew kept a secret, he kept it to protect someone. In this case, that someone had to be her. "You broke off our engagement to protect me, didn't you? What did you think you were protecting me *from?*"

A muscle twitched in his jaw. His dark eyes flashed with anger. "I gave up everything so you wouldn't find out. Everything."

"Jack, tell me." Britt's voice barely rose above a husky whisper.

He said nothing. He just stood there, staring at her, his jaw tight, his forehead creased in anguish.

The overpowering heat of him, the leather and musk scent of him, made her head whirl. Memories jumbled in her mind, but she held them back. She couldn't bear the pain. If she remembered how it felt to *have* these things, she'd have to remember how it felt to *lose* them.

Dear Harlequin Intrigue Reader,

Harlequin Intrigue serves up its romance with a generous dash of suspense, so sit back and feast on this month's selections!

Joanna Wayne continues her RANDOLPH FAMILY TIES miniseries with an exciting flourish in *A Mother's Secrets* (#577). Gayle Wilson brings another of her sexy, mysterious heroes to life in *Renegade Heart* (#578), the second title in her MORE MEN OF MYSTERY series. Look for the final installment in November.

We're delighted to introduce debut author Ann Voss Peterson and her book, *Inadmissible Passion* (#579). After someone tried to kill her, Brittany Gerritsen turned to the one man she vowed to stay away from—the man who called off their engagement. And our SECRET IDENTITY program heats up with *Little Boy Lost* (#580) by Adrianne Lee. When a look-alike impostor stole Carleen Ellison's identity and her sweet little boy, she had no choice but to turn to Kane Kincaid—her baby's secret father.

As always, Harlequin Intrigue is committed to giving readers the best in romantic suspense and that is a promise you can count on!

Sincerely,

Denise O'Sullivan
Associate Senior Editor
Harlequin Intrigue

INADMISSIBLE PASSION

ANN VOSS PETERSON

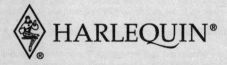

HARLEQUIN®

TORONTO • NEW YORK • LONDON
AMSTERDAM • PARIS • SYDNEY • HAMBURG
STOCKHOLM • ATHENS • TOKYO • MILAN • MADRID
PRAGUE • WARSAW • BUDAPEST • AUCKLAND

ISBN 0-373-22579-2

INADMISSIBLE PASSION

Copyright © 2000 by Ann Voss Peterson

This edition published by arrangement with Harlequin Books S.A.

® and TM are trademarks of the publisher. Trademarks indicated with
® are registered in the United States Patent and Trademark Office, the
Canadian Trade Marks Office and in other countries.

Visit us at www.eHarlequin.com

Printed in U.S.A.

ABOUT THE AUTHOR

Ever since she was a little girl making her own books out of construction paper, Ann Voss Peterson wanted to write. So when it came time to choose a major at the University of Wisconsin, creative writing was her only choice. Of course, writing wasn't a *practical* choice—one needs to earn a living. So Ann found jobs ranging from proofreading legal transcripts, to working with quarter horses, to washing windows. But no matter how she earned her paycheck, she continued to write the type of stories that captured her heart and imagination—romantic suspense. Ann lives near Madison, Wisconsin, with her husband, her toddler son, her border collie and her quarter horse mare.

Books by Ann Voss Peterson

HARLEQUIN INTRIGUE
579—INADMISSIBLE PASSION

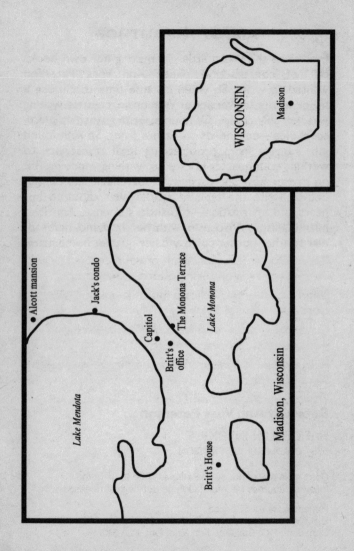

WISCONSIN

Madison

Lake Mendota

Alcott mansion

Jack's condo

Capitol

Britt's office

The Monona Terrace

Lake Monona

Britt's House

Madison, Wisconsin

CAST OF CHARACTERS

Brittany Gerritsen—She'll discover the truth about her friend's death, even if she must face the man she once loved in the courtroom.

Jackson Alcott—Five years ago he had to choose between Britt and a harmful secret. What will he do now?

Tangi Rowe—Someone tried to make her death look like an accident.

Grant Alcott—The suave senator seems genuinely upset about the dead woman.

Tia Alcott—Grant's wife repeats Grant's alibi a bit too glibly.

Roger Alcott—The patriarch of the Alcott family will do anything to keep their position in society.

Mimi Alcott—Her delicate health keeps son Jack close to the family.

Kimberly Alcott—Will Jack's sister's upcoming wedding get in the way of justice?

Kyle Ayers—Is Kimberly's fiancé trying to take Jack's place in the family?

Detectives Mylinski and Cassidy—The cops on the case.

Chapter One

Assistant District Attorney Brittany Gerritsen brushed her fingertips over her cheekbones and prayed the tracks of her tears weren't visible in the first glow of dawn. Striding past idling police cars and through crackling autumn leaves, she focused on the highway's guardrail. Twisted and mutilated, the metal gaped like a screaming mouth. She shuddered, but kept walking. "He won't get away with it, Tangi," she whispered. "I promise you that."

"I don't know who called you, Counselor, but it's just a car accident." At the sound of Detective Cassidy's nasal whine, Britt picked up her pace to avoid him.

No luck. He joined her, his strides keeping time with hers, his sweet aftershave choking the scent of autumn from the air. The red-and-blue lights of a half-dozen police cars pulsed off his face, giving his complexion a sickly gleam, like the scales of a dead fish. "Some babe drove Sugar Daddy's Porsche off the road. No need for a district attorney."

Pivoting to fully face him, she gestured to the unblemished asphalt. "If this is an accident, Detective, where are the skid marks?"

He shrugged. "Lots of accident scenes don't have skid marks. But if you don't like that scenario, try suicide. Crazy bitch decided to end it and didn't want to stop and explain."

Britt quelled the anger igniting in her belly. Dan Cassidy had to be the laziest, most disagreeable lout on the force. How he'd kept his job for the last twenty years was a mystery. How he'd made detective, she'd never know. "Guess again, Cassidy."

"What? A homicide? I should believe a husband or boyfriend gunned for the guardrail and jumped out at the last second?" His guffaw echoed in the gully below.

"Do me a favor and just follow procedure, Cassidy. It's a major crime scene until you find evidence to the contrary," she ordered, spinning away from him before she said something unprofessional.

To her relief, he didn't follow. She trudged alone to the edge of the steep bank. Below the ravaged guardrail, oak and hickory trees jutted from the early-morning fog. Yellow, brown and red-leafed branches clawed into the police spotlights' glare like frantic fingers. Beyond the web of rescue workers' ropes, the Porsche's hazy red form wrapped around a giant oak. Its white Wisconsin license plate reflected the police lights. The letters throbbed red, stinging the backs of Britt's eyes. S-U-M-B-O-D-Y.

Britt squeezed her eyes closed. Thunder rose in her ears. The vanity plate, the red Porsche—both gifts from a man who should have spent his money on his wife.

The man desperate to keep his affair with Tangi secret.

"Oh, Tangi," she whispered, "You didn't have to

try so hard to be somebody. You were always important to me.''

And she had been important. So important. Ever since Tangi had offered to share her craypas in Mrs. Ellison's third-grade class, she'd been there for Britt. Tangi was there with a toast when Britt graduated from law school. Tangi was there with a shoulder to cry on and a bottle of mind-numbing cognac on the awful night of Britt's engagement party.

Tangi had always been there. Always supportive. Never judgmental. God knew, Britt had tried her best to give her friend the same kind of acceptance, the same kind of unconditional love. And God knew she'd failed more than once. Now she wouldn't get another chance.

Britt tried to breathe, but her lungs constricted as if the breath had been knocked out of her. Cold wind buffeted her face and ripped several strands of hair from her tight chignon. The chill seeped through her trench coat and into her bones. Below, the police photographer snapped away, his flashbulb popping in the haze.

Slowly, the sun inched over the horizon. The deputy coroner started his climb back up the bank, puffing and wheezing like the overweight, three-pack-a-day smoker he was.

She nodded a greeting but remained rooted to her spot. She'd have time to discuss his findings later. Now she needed all her energy, all her resolve, to quell the sobs threatening to wrack her body.

The sun's rays reached into the ravine, burning away the last wisps of fog. Metal saws screeching, police and rescue workers cut away steel and pulled Tangi's body from the Porsche. The zip of the body bag echoed in Britt's mind, almost shredding all that remained of her self-control. She gasped for air.

When Dad had awakened her in the middle of the night saying he'd heard Tangi's license plate on his police scanner, she hadn't wanted to accept the inevitable. Now she couldn't deny it any longer. Tangi Rowe was dead. Cold tears trickled down Britt's cheeks and pooled under her chin. "Oh Tangi. Why didn't you stay away from him? Why wouldn't you listen to me?"

Detective Al Mylinski's heavy arm draped around her shoulders, warm and reassuring. "Talking to yourself is a bad sign."

She swallowed into an aching throat and dug in the pockets of her coat for a tissue. Finding none, she swiped at her eyes with the back of her hand.

"This will cure you." His pudgy fingers coaxed a hot foam cup into her fist.

The bracing aroma of his infamous battery-acid-blend coffee snapped her senses to life. She sipped the brew and turned to face the detective. "About time you got here."

What's this?" Mylinski raised his hand to touch her cheek. "The Ice Maiden is crying? Where are those blasted *State Journal* photographers when you need them? We got to document this. The boys downtown will never believe it."

Obviously, he wanted to make her feel better. But even in the face of his teasing, she couldn't bring herself to smile. She nodded toward the body bag the paramedics were loading into the ambulance. "My friend, Tangi Rowe."

"I know." Deep furrows of concern cut into Mylinski's balding brow. He patted her shoulder. "I'm sorry."

She waved his sympathy aside and swiped at the tears swamping her eyes. She didn't have time to waste on emotion right now. Later she could cry. Later she could mourn. Now she had to get control of herself. She had to do her job.

"That little worm, Cassidy, says you think this is a homicide."

She forced herself to focus on the evidence. "That's right."

"Can I ask why?"

"I just know, Al. It wasn't an accident. And I know it wasn't suicide."

Mylinski looked at her with the intense care he might grant a dying friend. "Can I ask how?"

Pain knotted her stomach and made her head spin. Her arms and legs grew heavy with a fatigue that was more than physical. A fatigue of the soul. "Because Tangi was pregnant, and she would never kill her baby. But I know who would."

Mylinski patted her shoulder a few more times. "If there's dirt to be found, you can bet a week of pay-days I'll find it. Just roll me in the right direction."

She nodded, but a shiver inside caused her to hesitate. Whether from fear of confronting Tangi's murderer, or his powerful family, she didn't know. She'd give almost anything to leave that particular door to the past closed, but she had no choice. It didn't matter how powerful his family was. It didn't matter who his brother was. He would pay for what he'd done.

She drew herself up to her full height. "Congressman Grant Alcott."

BRITT GLANCED down at her desk clock. Ten-thirty. Any minute now, Grant Alcott would walk through the door of her office, and she'd better be ready. She slipped a compact from her desk drawer and flipped it open. Studying her face in the tiny mirror, she flinched. Puffy shadows lurked under her eyes, dark as bruises in her Norwegian-fair skin. Her eyes contained as much red as blue, and her nose was so scarlet, it looked as if she'd spent the weekend either on the beach or in the bottle.

Losing her best friend in the world was almost more than she could take. But even though her emotions were more raw and shredded than fresh hamburger, she had to confront Grant Alcott. She must witness for herself the expression on his face when she accused him of murdering Tangi and his own unborn baby. Then she'd know. And once she knew, nothing could stop her from nailing his rotten hide to the wall.

Dabbing concealer and powder under her eyes and over her red nose, she rehearsed the words she planned to use to confront the congressman.

The bleat of the telephone interrupted her thoughts. She punched the speaker button. "Yes?"

"Ms. Gerritsen, Congressman Alcott and his attorney are here to see you."

"His attorney?" Britt snapped the compact shut and her pulse picked up its pace. When she'd called Grant's office, she'd asked to consult with him on a pending investigation. Any smart politician would bring an attorney, just in case.

Or was Grant's need for a lawyer more specific? She hadn't released news of Tangi's death, pending Tangi's mother's notification. Of course, reporters could have picked up that much listening to their police scanners. But they couldn't know Tangi was murdered. Only her murderer would know that. And he'd be prepared. "Send them in."

She looked up from her desk as Grant sauntered into her tiny office and flashed his golden-boy smile. No question what Tangi had seen in him. Besides his money and power, of course. From his tawny hair to his square shoulders, Congressman Alcott had been born with the all-American good looks any college quarterback would envy. The recent addition of gray at his temples gave him just the right touch of sophistication and sincerity. Knowing Grant, if nature hadn't provided him with the perfect amount of gray, a hair designer had.

"Hello, Britt. You're looking beautiful as ever." Grant's once-silken voice had grown rough with too many double scotches and hand-rolled cigars. A diamond-studded wedding band glittered from his left hand.

Trying not to grit her teeth, she rose and gave him a civilized nod. "Congressman. I hear you brought your law—" She swallowed the rest of her sentence as Jackson Alcott strode through the door.

Five years had passed since the awful night of their engagement party, but it might have been five minutes judging by the wave of pain that crashed over her. He looked different. Though his hair retained the dark luster she remembered so well, the planes of his face had sharpened, replacing all traces of youthful idealism with an air of power. Where his brother looked like the perpetual college boy, Jack was all man.

Of course she'd seen him during the past five years. Each time television cameras focused on a movie starlet accused of shooting her agent or a politician jailed for assaulting an aide, celebrity attorney Jackson Alcott seemed to be there, walking into the courtroom beside the accused. A hired gun in a thousand-dollar suit.

"Britt." The low rumble of his voice sent a shiver slinking up her spine.

"Jack," she managed to say. Her heart pounded like a judge's gavel, hammering high in her chest. After all these years, she'd convinced herself her wild attraction to him was dead, killed by his betrayal. Obviously, her body didn't agree.

Knees untrustworthy, she dipped to her chair. "Jack, Grant, please sit."

While Grant claimed one of the chairs in front of her desk, Jack remained standing, his restless gaze assessing the room.

What did he see? Britt followed his gaze, trying to view her office through his dark eyes. Her furniture consisted of vinyl-upholstered chairs and a desk that had been abused by generations of assistant district attorneys. No art. No character. Not even a window. Nothing to impress a man like Jack. She shifted in her chair. Her new gray suit pinched, as if she'd borrowed it from someone else.

She closed her eyes for a moment and shoved her insecurities aside. The Alcott family cared about expensive furniture and clothes, she didn't. She cared about sending scum like Grant Alcott to prison. And after this morning's meeting, she'd heap so much trouble on the sleazy congressman, even a highpowered snake like Jack couldn't slither him out.

"What is this meeting about, Counselor?" Jack

leaned against the doorjamb, folding his arms across his chest like an impatient king.

She met Jack's dark gaze. Her heart seemed to knock against her ribs even faster. "I have a few questions for your client. Since I doubt he wants the press to hear these questions, I thought it wise to meet here rather than at Grant's constituency office."

"Do we have to be so formal, Britt?" Grant asked, the chuckle in his voice grating on her nerves. He leaned back in his chair and smirked. "After all, we were almost family. Weren't we, Jack?"

Except for a slight twitch in his jaw, Jack remained stone-faced. Apparently, he didn't care about their past relationship. Maybe he never had.

Something close to sorrow rose in Britt's chest at the thought. She loved—no, *used* to love him with all her heart. But he hadn't shared her feelings. If he had, he never could have walked away like he did. He never could have been so cruel.

"You're so generous, Britt, to think of Grant's political career. The D.A.'s office is kinder and gentler than I realized. But since I don't see any members of the press hanging around at the moment, why don't you tell us why we're here?"

Britt straightened in her chair, her sorrow replaced by the slow burn of anger. She hadn't missed Jack's sarcasm and anti-establishment view of the world, that was for certain. Anti-establishment, what a laugh. Jack's family *owned* the establishment.

But they'd never own her.

She looked Grant straight in the eye. "When did you last see Tangi Rowe?"

"Tangi Rowe?" His eyebrows knitted as if he had

to search his memory. "Good-looking redhead, right? Isn't she an old friend of yours?"

He knew exactly who Tangi Rowe was. Who did he think he was kidding? "When did you last see her?"

"I remember meeting her at that engagement party the family threw for you and Jack." He paused as if waiting for a reaction from Jack. Getting none, he grinned and raised his hands from the chair arms, palms up. "She seemed friendly."

Anger hummed in Britt's ears. The engagement party. What a joke. Jack's parents had thrown the black-tie affair at the Maple Bluff Country Club. Champagne, a string quartet, and loads of pretension. That night, Jack's father had offered her an obscene amount of money to break the engagement. He needn't have bothered. Not only did she refuse him, but by the close of the evening, Jack had ended their relationship himself.

And more to the point, Tangi and Grant had been much more than friendly that night. "Yes, I remember. I interrupted the two of you out in the courtyard."

Grant shrugged, amused by her anger. "Oh, yeah. How could I forget? Tangi Rowe was quite—"

"Is there a point to this line of questioning, besides strolling down memory lane?" Jack looked at his watch. A plain little number. Not the Rolex watch she expected. He sighed. "Grant and I have busy schedules, Britt. Can we get on with it?"

Britt balled her hands into fists beneath her desk. Her heart still thrummed in her chest, but remnants of her desire for Jack were no longer the cause. "It seems you've been seeing a lot of Tangi in the last few months, Grant. There are witnesses.''

Watching Grant squirm to come up with an excuse gave Britt a certain amount of satisfaction. She hadn't found any witnesses. At least not yet. But Al Mylinski was canvassing Tangi's neighborhood this morning, so her statement wasn't all bluff.

Without looking, she felt Jack raise his brows. ''What interest does the District Attorney's office have in friends Grant may or may not have?''

Britt did her best to ignore Jack, focusing her attention on Grant. ''Tangi's carrying a child. Your child.''

''Did she—'' Grant closed his mouth, his gaze dropping to the nameplate on her desk.

Jack lunged forward, slamming his fist inches from her nameplate. ''What is this about?''

''Sit down, Jack.''

He shook off her order, leaning toward her over the desk. ''You and I have to talk. Grant, I'll meet you outside.''

Britt tore her gaze from Jack, fixing the force of her glare on Grant. ''Tangi's carrying your child, isn't she, Grant?''

Eyes downcast, he looked more like a boy caught stealing bubble gum than a congressman flirting with the end of his career. Finally, after fitting a polite smile on his face, Grant raised his eyes to meet hers. ''I think you're mistaken, Britt.''

Mistaken? Fat chance. Grant's expression the split second before his political instincts kicked in told her all she needed to know. Grant knew about his baby.

Jack moved in front of her, blocking her view of

his brother. "That's enough, Grant. Wait for me outside. I'll deal with this."

Adrenaline pumped through her like a jolt of espresso. She scrambled out of her chair and stretched to her full height. "Grant, sit."

Grant remained in his chair, amusement spreading across his face.

Jack glowered at her.

Too bad. He wasn't going to take away her chance to confront Grant. "This is official business and I want Grant to hear—"

"Official business? I haven't heard word one about a crime. This interview has nothing to do with Grant. Your problem is with me."

"With you? What are you talking about?" Did Jack think she'd arranged this meeting to get to him? The idea was ridiculous. Jack didn't work local cases. There wasn't enough money or serious crime in Madison to attract a big shot like Jack.

And Grant wasn't charged with anything—yet. Even if Jack did still live in Madison and teach at the University of Wisconsin law school when he wasn't involved in some headline-making case elsewhere, she had no reason to expect him to accompany Grant to this meeting. If she'd known, she would have found some other way to confront Grant—alone.

Jack circled the desk and stood close. Too close. Her senses reeled. He wore the same cologne, its musk-and-leather scent plunging her into memories she'd spent five long years struggling to forget. The warm whisper of his sheets against her skin on a snowy Saturday morning, the flavor of Pinot Noir sipped while wrapped in his arms, the hot stirring inside her when they kissed. She backed away.

"It's been five years, Britt. Can't you put the past behind you?"

Anger flared in the pit of her stomach. Jack thought she'd falsify an investigation for vengeance's sake. His arrogance knew no bounds. Sure, she'd love to pay him back for the way he'd treated her five years ago, but she'd never sacrifice her integrity to do so. She wouldn't sacrifice her integrity for *any* reason.

She swallowed hard. She couldn't let Jack get to her. She had to maintain control. She had to stay professional. "This interview is official. A crime *has* been committed."

Jack scrutinized her with those damn sexy eyes. "What crime?"

"Murder. Tangi was murdered last night."

"Mur—" Grant stopped short, sucking air. "Oh God."

For the first time since he'd walked through her door, Jack looked at his brother.

"Oh God," Grant repeated. He hunched over, clutching his middle as if he'd been shot. His face crumpled. "Tangi."

Britt couldn't move, couldn't speak. She could only stare like a gawker at the scene of a bloody accident. She'd expected cold denial. She'd expected a blink followed by a glib alibi. She'd expected anything but grief.

"Are you charging Grant with murder?"

She shook her head, buying time, hoping her voice wouldn't fail her. "Not at this time."

Jack bolted around the desk and grabbed Grant's arm. Pulling him to his feet, Jack yanked open the door. "In that case, my client has nothing more to say." He ushered his brother out of her office and slammed the door behind them, wood cracking against wood.

Britt dropped to her chair and tried to breathe. A tremble claimed her from the inside out. Not only had she allowed Jack to whisk Grant away before he'd answered her questions, but Grant's reaction to Tangi's death raised more doubts in her mind than it resolved.

She rested her head in her hands, her mind spinning. Was she wrong to suspect Grant? Had someone else killed Tangi?

She didn't know anymore.

But one thing was certain. If Grant *had* murdered Tangi, Britt had made a serious tactical error. This morning's meeting had accomplished nothing but to warn Grant she suspected him.

Damn Jack. She hadn't planned on him. His rebuke rang in her ears with each throb of her pulse. Only Jackson Alcott could believe she would throw her professionalism and integrity aside for vengeance.

Jack's integrity, Jack's honesty may be flexible, but hers wasn't. All she'd ever asked from anyone was the unvarnished truth. And she'd always responded with the same. Her suspicion of Grant had nothing to do with gaining vengeance for Jack's betrayal five years ago. Nothing.

She leaned back, forcing the breath in and out of her lungs. She had imagined running into Jack countless times since the night of their engagement party. She'd concocted numerous scenarios in her mind. In each, she had pictured herself wearing something beautiful and seductive, her hair cascading over her shoulders in rippling gold waves, her tongue witty and carefree. And Jack. She'd always imagined Jack being so struck by her, he couldn't help but see the horrible mistake he'd made five years ago, he couldn't help but apologize and beg for her forgiveness. And then she'd be able to tell him she didn't need him anymore. She didn't love him. He was too late to win her back. And the pain in his eyes would be her reward.

Never had she imagined their first meeting since their engagement party would go as badly as this.

She shoved her tangled thoughts of Jack aside. She had an investigation to run and a promise to keep. The only thing that truly mattered was the evidence. The evidence would point the way to the truth. The evidence would show whether Grant was guilty or innocent. She snatched her phone from its cradle.

"Yes?" her secretary answered.

"Maggie, I'd like you to call downstairs and leave a message for Detective Mylinski. I want to see him the second he returns."

"Will do, Ms. Gerritsen."

Britt hung up, her trembling easing somewhat, the empty ache inside her reduced to its familiar, bearable level again.

The evidence would tell the true story. The only story she wanted to hear.

Chapter Two

Jack drove in silence. Any words he tried to speak would probably come out in the form of an unintelligible bellow. He didn't dare glance at Grant slumped in the passenger seat beside him, staring out the window with unseeing eyes. He could throttle his brother. If not for Grant's obvious anguish over Tangi Rowe's death, he may have done just that the moment they left Britt's office.

He dug his fingers into the Jaguar's steering wheel. "Thanks for telling me Britt was the assistant D.A. you were meeting with." Not quite a bellow, but damn close.

Grant's gaze didn't wander from the window. "You wouldn't have come with me if I'd told you."

Jack suppressed a scoff. Of course he wouldn't have, regardless of his father's appeal on Grant's behalf. He should have heeded his misgivings when dear old Dad voiced his concern that a small matter with the D.A. could prevent Grant from attending his sister's prewedding luncheon. But Roger knew which buttons to push, and though Jack figured he was stepping into more than he bargained for, Kimberly's happiness had seemed worth the price at the time. So he'd agreed to smooth things over. For his sister's sake.

Smooth things over? What a laugh. Instead of a small matter, he'd encountered his ex-fiancée and a pending murder charge.

Of course he didn't believe for a minute Grant was guilty of murder. Adultery, on the other hand, was right up his brother's alley. Jack had headed off enough "small matters" to know. And he didn't have to stretch his imagination far to believe Grant had fathered an illegitimate child. But murder? Not a chance. Grant had neither the passion nor the guts to commit murder.

And just in case being roped into representing Grant on another of his self-destructive foul-ups wasn't bad enough, Jack now faced the prospect of confronting Britt on the other side of the courtroom.

Britt. His muscles tightened. She'd changed since the night of their engagement party. She'd grown harder, tougher. That's what working in the district attorney's office could do to a person. He'd seen it before. He just didn't like seeing it in Britt.

Her appearance hadn't changed. Neither had his physical response to her. Memories of her husky laugh, the ticklish spot at the nape of her neck, and the soul-shattering heat of her kisses made his muscles tense further.

Five years ago, she hadn't been tough enough. Far from it. And deep down, Jack knew the district attorney's office didn't deserve all the blame. His role in her transformation gnawed at him.

And those shreds of guilt were exactly why he couldn't be caught up in this. "I can't represent you, Grant."

"Can't or won't?"

"I *won't* represent you."

Grant shrugged as if Jack's refusal was merely hearsay. "You want out? Talk to the man in charge."

Jack barked out a short, hard laugh. Talk. He couldn't remember ever talking to their father. One only listened to Roger Alcott. Or yelled back. Over the years, Jack had become a master at yelling back.

Grant, on the other hand, never yelled back. He obeyed Roger's every command, lived out Roger's every ambition, and then sabotaged all he achieved with women and booze.

Jack drove past the Governor's mansion and swung into the curving cobblestone driveway of the Alcott house. His pulse picked up its pace. He looked forward to having a chat with dear old Dad. Roger wasn't going to get his way this time. Jack parked the Jag and preceded Grant in their march to the front door.

Jack hated this house. He hated the unyielding stone facade. He hated the staunch pillars. But most of all, he hated the suffocating pressure that assaulted his chest the moment he approached the threshold. Even the bracing scent of Lake Mendota and the crisp essence of maple leaves carried in the October wind couldn't rip through the tension that cloaked the house.

What he wouldn't give to be up north right now for the opening of the Bonanza. It had taken him years to plan the Bonanza Boys' Ranch and make it a reality. And now that he'd finally finished hiring counselors and handing out scholarships to at-risk teenagers, he'd had to miss opening day to deal with

Grant's problem. Well, he wouldn't miss tomorrow. He'd be driving up the interstate before sundown.

He threw open the door and strode into the marble-floored entry hall. The aroma of rich food filled the hall, mixing with the scent of vase after vase of his mother's favorite pink roses. Fresh flowers, of course. A touch Mom would insist on for Kimberly's luncheon. His watch read eleven-thirty. The family would be gathering in the dining room.

Without a word, Grant left Jack, heading for the sweeping staircase and probably the third-floor suite he shared with his wife, Tia, when they weren't in Washington. Leave it to Grant to duck out of a confrontation. Especially when it concerned him.

Jack followed the subdued feminine voices drifting from the dining room. The sooner he faced Roger, the sooner he could hit the highway. And the sooner he could push the memory of Britt's sweet face from his mind.

He stepped into the dining room, his shoes sinking into the plush carpeting as if mired in quicksand.

Kimberly and Tia glanced up from a bottle of red wine, one half-filled glass, and stacks of photographs spread across a side table.

"Jackson, I didn't know you were coming to the luncheon." Kimberly bounced from her chair and trotted across the room toward him. She spread her arms and wrapped him in a hug. "I'll have the caterer set another place."

Tall with long dark hair, Kimberly possessed a single-minded intensity similar to his own. Lately her intensity focused like a laser on her fiancé, Kyle Ayres, and the final details of their wedding.

"Sorry, Kim. I'm not staying."

She pulled back, studying his face. "Why—"

"I'm here to see our father."

Her happy expression drooped. "Not now, Jackson. I need Daddy."

"It won't take long." He wouldn't let it.

Kimberly wrinkled her nose. Apparently, she didn't believe him.

"It's important. I have to talk to him about Grant."

"Grant? What about Grant?" Tia Alcott leaped to her feet, sloshing wine over the lip of her glass. "If something's happened to Grant, I deserve to know."

"He's upstairs," Jack said, avoiding her question. He'd never liked his sister-in-law. Her benign smile and phony concern for housing the unfortunate rubbed him the wrong way. She reminded him of the colorful tapestry tote bag she carried everywhere, beautiful and elaborate on the surface, but underneath an unattractive tangle of threads.

Spoiled, self-centered, and shallow, she'd come from a family with ample prestige and meager wealth. She offered Grant respectability, and he supplied her with cash. A match made in heaven.

Tia raked her black bobbed hair off her forehead and took a long sip of wine. Something akin to fear consumed her dark eyes. Did Tia know about Grant's affair with Tangi? Did she know about the baby? Or about Tangi's death?

Tia clicked her blood-red talons against her wineglass. "I have to go talk to Grant." Clutching her bag in one hand and her wine bottle and glass in the other, she almost flew into him, dropping the bag at his feet.

Not yet noon and his sister-in-law was already half loaded on expensive wine. Hell, who could blame her? How many "small matters" could a wife be expected to overlook without drowning her sorrows in a bottle? After she learned about the latest, she'd need more than a bottle. She'd need an entire winery.

Jack stooped to pick up the tapestry bag. Grabbing the smooth leather handle, he delivered it into Tia's hands.

Tia snatched it from him without a whisper of thanks and dashed out the door.

Kimberly let out a frustrated groan. "Jack, what's this all about?"

Guilt twinged his conscience. For someone who wanted to safeguard Kimberly's luncheon, he was doing a damn poor job. "Tell you later, Kimberly. Where's Roger?"

Hands on hips, she glared at him. "Every time you talk to Daddy it turns into a fight."

True enough. But Jack wasn't about to start following Roger's orders to keep the peace. "I'll try to control the hemorrhaging this time. Where is he?"

"Mother is in the kitchen."

"I don't want to talk to Mother. Where's Roger?"

"Jackson," a deep voice rasped from behind him. Jack turned.

Tall, slim and white-haired, Roger Alcott stood strapping strong, tough as steel wire. He walked with purpose, he sat with purpose, he even slept with purpose. He had big dreams, and he insisted his children fulfill them. "We'll discuss this in my study."

Offering an apologetic glance to his sister, Jack followed Roger down the hall. Paneled in knotty pine and furnished in leather, Roger's study had a distinctively masculine air. Elaborate models of semi trucks and other mementos of the trucking empire he'd built from scratch glittered between book-lined shelves.

Wood blinds masked the floor-to-ceiling windows, permitting only slivers of sunlight to enter the room. An oversized fireplace yielded heat, light, and the strong scent of burning wood. An oppressive odor when not out in the open air, especially when blended with the fog of Roger's cigars.

Roger strode to the elaborate wet bar and grabbed a bottle of fine whiskey from the shelf. He splashed the alcohol into three tumblers and thrust one of them at Jack.

Jack held up a hand. "No thanks. I don't hit the hard stuff quite this early."

"You look as if you need it." Roger pushed the glass into his palm.

Jack fingered the cold crystal but didn't drink. He nodded to the third tumbler. "Expecting someone?"

"Kyle will be joining us as soon as he placates his bride-to-be."

Jack frowned. Kimberly's future husband was a lawyer of some repute. Undeserved, in Jack's opinion. But as in everything else, Jack's opinion differed greatly from his father's. Kyle had earned a special place in Roger's heart with the enthusiastic way he kissed the royal Alcott feet.

Jack raised an eyebrow. "You can't face me without your yes-man present?"

Roger's chortle grated like a rasp drawn across a tin can. "Your success has gone to your head, my boy. You'll do well to remember your place in the family."

Always the family. Jack's first memories were of Roger upbraiding him about the family and his place in it. "You'd never let me forget."

Jack looked down at the whiskey in his hand. Truth

was, after this morning's meeting, he could use a drink before dealing with his father. But if he turned to the bottle every time he butted heads with Roger, he'd have landed in the drunk tank long ago. He set the glass on the bar.

The door inched open and Kyle Ayres slipped inside. Very stylish with his slicked-back blond hair and wire-rimmed glasses, Kyle had little substance. He reminded Jack of a male model in a magazine ad, handsome veneer but lacking inside. But one thing Kyle didn't lack was money. A specialist in white-collar criminal law, Kyle seemed to be on his way to the top. And that one commodity, coupled with Roger's approval, qualified him to marry Kimberly Alcott.

Besides the fact that Jack's little sister adored Kyle.

And that was the most perplexing thing of all. Kyle was handsome and rich all right, but he wasn't nearly good enough for Kimberly. Some day she'd realize it. Jack hoped that day came before she said "I do."

Roger handed Kyle the third tumbler. Accepting it with a slight nod of his head, Kyle backed into the shadows where he would watch and listen as usual, until Roger needed his support.

At least Kyle's silence made him easy to ignore. Jack shifted his focus back to Roger. The sooner he got this over, the sooner he could get out of here. "Grant may be in serious trouble this time."

Roger dismissed his words with a wave of his hand. "Nothing the family can't handle."

The family again. "That's what I want to discuss with you. Grant needs another attorney. Someone impartial. Someone who isn't family. I'll have my secretary assemble a list of good lawyers this afternoon."

"Someone who isn't family? You know that's not the way we do things, Jackson."

"Maybe the way we Alcotts do things is the reason Grant's in this mess."

Roger ignored the jab. Typical. "What the hell did the D.A. want with Grant?"

Jack leaned against the bar. In Roger's mind, Grant's problems stemmed from outsiders plotting to destroy a potentially great political leader. They had nothing to do with Grant or the family who protected him at every turn. Roger believed that if the family stayed together and followed his direction, they could bulldoze their way through any obstacles Grant might face on his road to the Governor's mansion. And eventually, the White House. After all, the strategy had worked when Roger slashed his own road through the jungle of the trucking business.

But it wouldn't work against a murder charge. "Grant has been carrying on an affair with Tangi Rowe."

"Tangi Rowe? Do I know that name?"

Jack didn't answer. Roger had an uncanny memory for names, a trait which had served him well in business dealings. He remembered Tangi Rowe. This forgetful act was merely a ploy to introduce Britt into the conversation. And the last person Jack wanted to discuss with his father was Britt. "Grant got Tangi pregnant."

Roger's eyebrows rose. He paced across the floor, stopping to face the gaping fireplace. "Find out how much she wants."

"I'll talk to her this afternoon, sir," Kyle volunteered from his spot in the shadows.

Jack almost laughed. Just like his father to believe

a fat check could solve any problem. "It's not that easy."

"Nonsense. Grant and Tia have been trying to have a child for years. They can raise the baby as their own."

Eyeing his father's back, Jack shook his head. He could almost hear the gears turning in that cold-blooded political mind. Children are good for a politician's image. So why not buy Grant's own child?

Well, the Alcott wealth couldn't buy a resolution to this problem. "Tangi is dead. Grant is under investigation for her murder."

Roger stiffened. "How did they—" He stopped midsentence and gulped his whiskey, leaving Jack to wonder what he was about to say.

Silence blanketed the room, broken only by the resonant tick of the old grandfather clock and the shuffling of Kyle's Guccis.

Roger turned from the fire, his features shadowed against the flame's glow. "Who's in charge of the investigation?"

Apprehension crept up Jack's spine. If Grant knew Britt called the meeting, so did Roger. "You already know who's in charge. So why the question-and-answer session?"

Roger nodded. "What's her price?"

Jack straightened, temples throbbing. Roger's gall never ceased to amaze him. "She doesn't have a price. That's why you didn't want her in the family, remember?"

"Maybe she doesn't, but her father does."

Jack balled his hands into fists. Roger's threats of five years ago drummed in his memory. "How dare—'' He bit his tongue and forced himself to breathe deeply.

He couldn't let Roger see how important Britt still was to him. How he missed her honesty and razor-sharp wit. How he dreamed about her husky laugh on lonely nights. How no other woman had quite measured up.

If Roger knew, he would use Jack's memories against him like a gun pressed to his temple, hammer cocked. He'd done it before. "I'm driving back to the Bonanza this afternoon. I'll have my secretary fax over that list."

Roger's cheeks flamed, an artery in his neck bulging. "You will do nothing of the kind. Your ranch be damned. You will stay and support the family."

Kyle stepped behind Roger, a show of solidarity.

Jack quelled the anger pulsing in his ears. Time to try logic. "There's a major tactical downside to my representing Grant."

Roger reached into his breast pocket and pulled out one of his infernal cigars. "I'm listening."

"If we end up going to trial, a jury will likely believe I'm representing Grant because he's my brother, not because I'm convinced he's innocent."

"And what will a jury believe if you don't represent him? You're not just some public defender hanging around the courthouse steps. You're the top criminal lawyer in the whole damn country. The jury, the media, and the voters in Grant's district are going to think you distanced yourself because he's guilty."

Running the stogie beneath his nose, Roger inhaled deeply. "It's settled then. You *will* represent Grant, and Kyle here will act as second chair. If something goes wrong and Grant has to go to trial, I want you two to be ready.''

''Yes, sir.'' Kyle looked as if he might salute.

Disgust churned in Jack's gut. Roger had found himself the perfect surrogate son, all right. He hoped they would be very happy together, because there wasn't a chance in hell Jack was going along with Roger's plan. Another attorney could protect Grant. An attorney without the baggage Jack carried. ''You can either use my recommendations to find a new attorney or handle the matter yourself. I'll be up at the Bonanza.'' He spun on his heel and strode to the door.

''It's that woman, isn't it?''

Jack froze.

''That Gerritsen woman. You don't want to oppose her in court.''

An ache like an old football injury throbbed in Jack's back and shoulders. He turned to face Roger. ''That's ridiculous.''

''Is it?'' Roger rolled the cigar in his fingers. Shadow cloaked his eyes, but Jack knew he was watching, dissecting, looking for weakness. ''You don't have to worry about her, Jackson. Damage control is my first order of business. If she can't be persuaded to pursue other suspects, she won't be in charge of the investigation very long.''

In other words, if Britt didn't back off, Roger would ruin her career. He could do it too, of this Jack had no doubt. Campaign contributions were a precious commodity to any politician. And Roger contributed heavily to District Attorney Neil Fitzroy's campaign. A few persuasive words from Roger, and

Fitzroy would yank Britt from the case. Or send her to the unemployment line.

Roger's lips turned up in a sly grin. "However, if you stick with Grant, it might be wise to leave her in charge. You've always been able to influence the woman."

Futility settled into his bones like a long, drab winter. If Jack let him, Roger would use his threats against Britt and her family to control him until the end of time. "Your threats won't work this time, Roger. I don't have a relationship with Britt Gerritsen anymore, remember? I gave up everything five years ago. Everything. You've bled me dry. So like it or not, I'm off Grant's case."

The door swung open. "Grant's case?" a delicate feminine voice repeated.

Jack swung around and met his mother's worried hazel eyes.

Frail in a ruffled creation of fabric resembling peach-colored tissue, her skin held the pallor of long-suffered illness. "What kind of case is Grant involved in?"

"Nothing that matters, Mother." She doted on her younger son. She beamed with his accomplishments and suffered with his difficulties. Grant had given her plenty of cause for suffering. The last thing Jack wanted was to worry her further.

"Oh, Jackson. If Grant is in trouble—"

"He's not, Mother." Not yet. No point in worrying her unless murder charges were filed.

Roger stepped toward her. "We'll handle this, Mimi."

She held her ground. "We're talking about my son here. I have a right to know if he's in trouble."

Roger half sneered. "It's that Gerritsen woman. She's after the family. She wants to charge Grant with murder."

"Murder?" Blood drained from her already pale cheeks.

Jack dashed to her side and slipped an arm around her shoulders to steady her. Damn Roger. Charges might never be filed. Telling her only served to upset her. In her poor health, upsetting news could have serious repercussions. "It'll be all right, Mother."

She raised her chin, the worry lines in her forehead softening. "Of course. You'll take care of Grant like you always do, won't you, Jackson?"

Jack's stomach clenched.

"Won't you?"

Jack touched his fingers to her cheek. So cold and fragile. He could stand against his father, fight him blow for blow. But one look from his mother, one pleading word, and he caved. "Of course, Mother. I'll take care of everything."

BRITT REACHED for the foam cup Al Mylinski offered, steam rising into the cold evening air. The coffee was thicker than crude oil and smelled like burned rubber. But she'd had one hell of an afternoon in court, and she could use the caffeine to get through the evening. She choked down several gulps. "Great stuff as always, Al."

Mylinski walked beside her down the steps of the City County Building, Tangi's already-thick file tucked under his arm. The sun's twilight glow had nearly faded, and globe-shaped lights lit the walkway leading to the Monona Terrace. Britt had asked the detective to meet her outside. After spending the day cooped up in a windowless courtroom, memories of Jack plaguing her mind, she needed a breath of fresh air.

Mylinski chuckled. "Most people complain my coffee's too strong."

"No kidding?"

"Swear to God." His mouth contorted into a crooked grin. "Now I could stroll and chat about coffee for hours, but I know that's not why you wanted to see me. What's up?"

Britt tightened the belt of her trench coat with her free hand. "Have you found enough evidence to arrest Grant Alcott?"

"Depends."

"On what?"

"On whether you're forcing evidence to fit a story, or letting the evidence tell its own story."

She groaned. Cops could be so frustrating. Although she'd been raised by one, she still didn't understand how a cop's mind worked. "That didn't come out right. I'm not trying to railroad Grant. I want to find the truth, same as you. So why don't you tell me the story you've uncovered."

Mylinski handed her his coffee cup and flipped open the file's cover, clutching the contents tightly in the cool breeze. "The autopsy report won't be along for a while, but I sat through it this afternoon, and I got my notes here." He fished out a notebook and stuck the rest of the file back under his arm.

She glanced at the open notebook in his hand. All she could make out was a haphazard tangle of squiggles.

Under normal circumstances, she would have attended the autopsy. But nothing was normal about this case. The thought of Tangi's autopsy sent a clammy shiver slithering over her skin that had nothing to do with the chill of the wind. She struggled to find her voice. "You know I can't read your writing. Paraphrase for me."

"Davis did the autopsy. He fixed the time of death at midnight, give or take half an hour. Tangi Rowe was beat up an hour or two before she died. Beat up bad."

The lights of the Terrace blurred. Britt swallowed and opened her eyes wide to keep the tears from trickling down her cheeks.

"Davis says she probably wasn't conscious when her car went over the embankment. She died instantly when she hit the tree."

Britt stopped walking and closed her eyes. Images of her friend ripped through her mind. Tangi beaten. Tangi unconscious. Tangi dead.

"Sorry," Mylinski's gruff voice intruded.

Summoning her strength, Britt opened her eyes and nodded for him to continue.

"She was beat up in her apartment. We found blood—" He stopped, watching for Britt's reaction.

She waved him on, not trusting her voice.

"It seems the perpetrator loaded her into the car and took her out where we found her."

Britt drew in a deep breath and set her chin, locking her pain deep within her heart. This was not the time for emotion. If she wanted to keep her promise to Tangi, she needed to focus on the evidence. She handed his coffee back to him and resumed walking, her heels clicking determinedly on the concrete. "What else did you find at the scene?"

"One set of footprints in the mud."

"Footprints?"

"Men's dress shoes. Expensive."

Expensive. The type of shoes Grant would wear. Britt quickened her pace, striding through a gate and up one of the ramps leading to the Terrace's view of Lake Monona. "We'll need enough evidence for a search warrant."

Mylinski followed a half step behind, his sigh of frustration audible over the lap of the waves and the hum of the nearby traffic. No doubt he thought she was jumping to conclusions again. "We also found some fibers and other trace evidence on the body and the interior of the car. The lab says it'll take some time to analyze."

She nodded, more to herself than to Mylinski. Trace evidence always took time, and often it didn't add up to much. "What did you find in Tangi's apartment?"

"Besides the blood, we found some fingerprints we're trying to identify. And we found signs of a struggle."

Reaching the Otis Redding memorial bench overlooking Lake Monona, Britt sat down. Her legs hadn't stopped trembling since her run-in with Jack this morning, and the cold cement felt good through her coat. Like the cold slap of truth.

Concentrating, she closed her eyes and tried to imagine what had happened the night Tangi was murdered. She forced herself to think over the evidence, each piece bringing the picture into sharper focus. In her mind's eye, she saw the perpetrator beat Tangi, load her limp body into her Porsche, drive to the country road, send the car over the edge, and jump to safety. Each time she scrolled the images through her mind, the face of the killer was Grant's.

Mylinski sat beside her and took a long slurp from his coffee cup. "If the guy planned it, I wouldn't expect to see so much sloppy evidence. You know, the footprint and the blood. Also, he didn't need to move the body and stage the accident when we could see it was murder from the get-go. Only panic would drive someone to such extremes."

Exactly. Britt thought of Grant's reaction in her office. At the time, she had interpreted his display of emotion as grief. But what if she had read him wrong? What if his reaction was something else all together? "You said there were signs of struggle, right?"

Mylinski nodded. "Lamps tipped over, that kind of thing."

Britt added that to the picture in her mind. She took a deep breath. Time to try out her theory. "What if Grant and Tangi argued and he turned violent? The press would have a field day. Can you imagine the headlines? Congressman beats pregnant mistress. So what would Grant do? Stage the car accident as a cover-up. Or call his father to bail him out, and Roger stages the car accident. Either way, Grant is responsible."

Mylinski grunted. He fiddled with the brown polyester tie that drooped over his belly like a damp dish towel. His skepticism hung in the air like a bad odor.

Evidence. She needed evidence to bolster her theory. "Did you check the redial feature on Tangi's telephone?"

A cloud darkened Mylinski's balding brow. "Forget about the redial."

Forget about it? The feature stored the last number

dialed into the phone. If that number belonged to the Alcott estate, she would be on her way to proving her theory. "Why forget the redial?"

Mylinski's brow furrowed. Obviously, he had more bad news. "Cassidy was the first to check out the apartment. He used the phone to call for evidence technicians."

Britt couldn't believe her ears. "He erased the redial?"

"Yup."

Dan Cassidy again. She shouldn't be surprised. The county was filled with good, smart, competent police detectives, and she had to deal with Hopalong Cassidy. If she ever found enough evidence to bring Grant to trial, Jack would make mincemeat out of Cassidy on the witness stand.

Jack. She'd have to assemble a killer of a case to go up against Jack in the courtroom. A killer case. She could picture him now, his voice arching with passion and fire as he addressed the jury, his hand raised in the air as if swearing to God his client had been wronged.

She'd watched him in action many times in the years they were together. And while his courtroom technique had always engendered her respect, it had also inspired such a primitive ache of yearning inside her that it threatened to steal her self-control.

She bit her lip. Five years had failed to erase one detail about him from her memory. Just as five years had failed to lessen the pain of his betrayal the horrible night of their engagement party.

She forced her attention back to the case. If she was going to beat Jack in court, she had to support her theory with cold hard facts. "There must be some evidence pointing in Grant's direction."

Mylinski shook his head. "So far we've found nothing. Nada. In fact, Cassidy found a cab driver who picked Grant up here at this very convention center at eleven that night and drove him to the family home in Maple Bluff."

Britt's chest tightened. She shook her head in confusion. An alibi? Grant couldn't have an alibi. Could he? "Maybe he didn't stay home. Maybe he just picked up his car and drove over to Tangi's. Just because he went home doesn't mean he stayed there."

"His wife says different."

"Tia? What did she say?"

Mylinski fished in his file folder, pulling out a witness statement. "She said, 'I was with Grant all night. At the Monona Terrace Convention Center for a fundraiser and then at home.'"

Britt shook her head. "That doesn't mean anything, Al. I know Tia Alcott. She'd lie about what she ate for breakfast. She'd certainly lie to provide Grant with an alibi."

Mylinski coughed. He touched his throat with his fingertips. "Sorry. Must be coming down with something."

The only thing Mylinski was coming down with was lack of insight. "It's possible, Al. You've got to admit, things could have happened that way."

He reached into his pocket and pulled out a handful of Jolly Rancher candies. "Want one?"

She clenched her fists in her lap. "I'm not ignoring other suspects. I'm just asking you not to discount Grant this early in the investigation."

He unwrapped the cellophane and popped a pink

candy into his mouth. The scent of sugary watermelon clouded the air.

She swallowed, the smell making her a little queasy. "It could have happened just the way I said. Trust me. I've presented a lot of cases like this."

"You may be the one presenting the case, but I'll be the one up on the witness stand with his pants down. In all my years, I've never been accused of rushing to judgement and ignoring evidence, and I ain't going to leave myself open now."

She held up her hands, palms facing him. The last thing she wanted was to get Mylinski's back up. She needed an ally on the police force. Besides, he was her friend. And right now, she needed all the friends she could get. "All I'm saying is this cab driver and Tia don't necessarily provide Grant with an alibi for the time of the murder."

"They force me to look for more likely suspects. And unless some new evidence comes to light, that's what I'm going to do." He sucked hard on the candy. "I know this thing with Tangi stinks, and you have your reasons for suspecting Grant Alcott. But I won't let your feelings get in the way of my investigation."

Mylinski's words landed hard, like a kick in the head. Britt swallowed her frustration and forced a nod. He was right. She had to control her emotions. If she didn't, District Attorney Fitzroy would reassign the case before she could blink. If he wasn't so engrossed in the upcoming election, he probably would have reassigned Tangi's case already. "I agree. We have to look into every possibility."

He settled back on the bench, but the frown creasing his brow didn't disappear.

So he didn't buy her acquiescence. Well, he could think what he wanted. Nothing had changed her suspicion that Grant caused Tangi's death. If she had to, she would investigate him on her own.

Chapter Three

"May I help you, ma'am?"

Britt nodded to the prim wedding consultant, the same consultant who'd helped her begin planning her own ill-fated wedding five years ago. The woman hadn't changed a bit. She flashed Britt the same prissy smile and fingered the same gold reading glasses that dangled around the same loose-skinned neck. "I was told I could find Kimberly Alcott here. She has an appointment this morning."

The woman's face brightened. Amazing the effect the Alcott name had on people. "She and her matron of honor are upstairs in the Crystal Room trying on their headpieces. I can show you the way."

"That's all right. I know the way." She could do without an escort. No telling what kind of reception Kimberly and Tia would give her. If they reacted negatively, this woman wouldn't hesitate to remove Britt from her treasured clients' presence.

The woman nodded, and Britt walked across the lobby alone, the plush baby-blue carpet sucking at the heels of her pumps. Cherie's House of Bridals was just as Britt remembered: dramatic, opulent, intimidating. From urns of rose-scented potpourri, to ornate crystal chandeliers dripping from the ceiling, to the lush folds of silk and lace adorning each mullioned window, everything screamed wealth and social standing.

She mounted the sweeping staircase to strains of music so soothing, elevator music seemed raucous by comparison.

An unnatural tightness pinched her throat. She hadn't liked this place five years ago, and she liked it less now. Jack's mother had been the one who'd insisted she use Cherie's. Only the best befitted an Alcott union.

But she wasn't here to reminisce. If she struck fast, she could determine if Grant's alibi was genuine before the Alcott family circled their wagons.

Kimberly Alcott had always been friendly and might talk if she hadn't been warned to keep her mouth shut. But Britt's interest centered on Kim's matron of honor. Grant's wife, Tia.

Approaching the Crystal Room, Britt paused as two uniformed consultants shut the door behind them and strolled to the stairs. Apparently, they'd been dismissed. Perfect. If she could avoid a shouting match with the ever-volatile Tia, maybe she could get some answers before the consultants came back.

Britt rapped on the white door.

"Come in," a female voice called from inside.

Britt swung the door open. The room hadn't changed since the day she'd tried on one elaborate white satin concoction after another. The huge crystal chandelier still hung from the ceiling's center, sending droplets of light showering off mirrored walls in blinding prisms. And tension still seemed to hang in the air.

"What the hell are you doing here?" Tia sprang from the blue velvet love seat. She surged forward, nearly upsetting a small table set with a bottle of red wine and canapés. A glass of wine sloshed in one bejeweled fist.

Kimberly's reflection stared from the mirror, her forehead creased with shock and confusion, the veil embracing her guileless face in a halo of tulle and lace. "Britt? What *are* you doing here?"

Britt didn't have a chance to speak before Tia advanced. She stormed toward Britt, tromping across the lace edge of Kimberly's veil. "I'll tell you what she's doing here. She's trying to destroy our lives."

Tia raised her chin and tossed her cropped black hair. Although not as tall as Britt and Kimberly, she did a respectable job of peering down her nose. Of course, she'd practiced extensively. "My husband didn't kill the bitch, Miss Gerritsen. But I'm glad someone did."

Shock and horror streaked Kim's delicate features. Turning, she snatched Tia's arm.

Tia wrenched her arm from Kim's grip, her wineglass plummeting to the floor and bouncing off a tapestry tote bag. The blood-red liquid seeped into the carpet's thick pile.

Britt stepped back for safety's sake. So much for keeping Tia calm. Too much wine and her hatred for Tangi had Tia careening out of control.

Britt glanced at the door. Maybe she could use Tia's outburst to her advantage. She'd better hurry. Once the wedding consultants returned, they'd take one look at Tia's inflamed face and throw Britt out on her ear. "Tangi wasn't trying to destroy Grant. She loved him."

"Love?" Tia sneered. "Do you blackmail someone you love?"

Blackmail? Britt's heart pumped adrenaline. Would Tangi have stooped to blackmail? Much as Britt wanted to deny the charges, she couldn't. Tangi would have done almost anything if she was desperate enough. Her pregnancy might have pushed her over that line.

Blackmail was a strong motive for murder. "What was she blackmailing him about?"

Tia pursed her scarlet lips together, enmity stealing across her face. "I'm glad someone killed your sleazy friend. You're crazy if you think I'm going to help you fry my husband for it." Chin held high and eyes shooting daggers, Tia Price Alcott looked more than glad. She looked capable of killing Tangi herself.

Hot anger rose in Britt's throat. She swallowed. She'd come to discredit Grant's alibi, not get in a brawl with his wife. Tia had already slipped up once with her blackmail comment. With Tia's self-control out the window, maybe Britt could push hard enough to make her slip again.

She cleared her throat, considering her next question. "What time did Grant get home on Sunday night?"

Tia raked her talons through her hair. "I already told the police I was with Grant all night. At the Monona Terrace Convention Center and then at home. Now get out, or I'll have you thrown out."

Britt barely prevented the elation from showing on her face. "A cab drove Grant home from the Monona Terrace. He was quite alone."

A brittle smile tweaked Tia's lips. Her eyes glistened with indignation. "Besides driving home separately, we were together all night long and you can't prove otherwise. Now get the hell out of here!'' Her screech bounced off the mirrored walls.

Britt cringed. The wedding consultants would have to be deaf to miss that shriek. ''Kim? Did you see Grant that night?''

Kim stared wide-eyed at Britt. ''Kyle's car broke down. I left the house to pick him up and find a garage to fix it.''

''Did you see Grant before you left or after you returned?''

The door burst open and three women in black uniforms rushed into the room.

The interview was obviously over. She hadn't gotten all the information she'd hoped for, but it would have to be enough. Britt held up her hands in front of her. ''I was just leaving, ladies.''

SHIFTING ON THE hard chair, Jack stared out the steamy window at people shuffling by on the street outside. Years had passed since he'd last sat in the sweltering confines of the Easy Street Café. To his dismay, the place hadn't changed one bit. Fumes of burnt coffee, grilled grease, and sautéed cigarette butts still stung his eyes. Clattering dishes and shouted obscenities still assaulted his ears. And thoughts of Britt still crowded his mind.

He could imagine her sitting across the scarred table, nose buried in a legal file, lunching on coffee and blueberry bagels. Back then, this dump had seemed more bearable.

He picked up his cup and sipped. He hadn't come here to stroll down memory lane, and he certainly hadn't come for this insult to coffee. He'd come to confront Britt, to force her to stop badgering his family. How to accomplish this, he didn't know. But the words would come to him. They always did.

A dull chime and refreshing gush of cold air forewarned him. He glanced up in time to see the lunch crowd of cops and blue-collar workers shift to allow the door enough space to swing open.

Britt stepped inside. Cheeks pink from the brisk wind, she clutched her coat at her throat, hiking the hem just enough to show a glimpse of one long leg.

The glimpse of leg wasn't wasted on Jack. He allowed his gaze to saunter over the delicate ankle and up the shapely calf to where her leg disappeared under folds of her charcoal trench coat. He swallowed, throat tight. Seeing Britt had always sent his blood racing. That much hadn't changed.

Slipping a finger under his collar, he loosened his starched white shirt. This place had lousy ventilation. Someone should notify the Board of Health.

A couple of the cops nodded a greeting in her direction. She nodded back, pursing her lips in an expression that fell short of a smile. Glancing around the café for a vacant table, she spotted him. Her eyes grew wide. "Jack."

Her icy glare galvanized him like a cold slap in the face. He nodded to her with the same civility the cops had used. "Britt."

Strolling toward his table, she slipped off her leather gloves finger by finger like a siren in an old movie and stowed them in her coat pocket. "This place is a little low-rent for you, isn't it, Jack? I assume you're here to see me."

Jack resisted the urge to look her up and down. He couldn't allow a great pair of legs to muddle his brain.

"No. I'm here for the exceptional cuisine and atmosphere."

"I usually don't take plea bargains until charges are filed. But for you, I'll make an exception."

"Do you usually require evidence to file charges, or are you making that exception for me, too?"

She rapped the heel of one pump on the worn linoleum like the staccato tap of a blacksmith's hammer. "I meet with defense counsel in my office, not on my lunch hour. Call my secretary for an appointment."

She spun away from him and strode to the counter. Back rigid, she ordered coffee and a blueberry bagel in clipped tones loud enough to transcend the dull roar of the café crowd.

Leave it to Britt to give as good as she got. She had guts, he'd give her that. He'd always admired the way she'd stood up to Roger. Dear old Dad could be intimidating even on his gentler days, but he hadn't cowed Britt. No matter how he'd tried.

She had guts. And *that* was the quality that stirred his blood. His short exchange with her had it whipped into a froth.

But he couldn't let old feelings cloud his thinking. He had to stay on his toes around her if he was going to convince her to leave the family alone. At least until after Kimberly's wedding. He sipped his burned coffee and waited. Soon Britt's insatiable curiosity would get the better of her, and she'd return to his table. She could never leave without knowing why he'd come.

It didn't take long. After paying for her lunch, she returned to his table and sat opposite him. "Why are you here?"

Direct as always. "I heard you were shopping for wedding dresses this morning."

Britt finally smiled. Not a friendly smile. "I want to be prepared. No telling when I might meet a potential husband who isn't under his father's thumb. A man who knows how to keep a promise."

Her words stung like driving sleet against bare skin. But always a good lawyer, he knew when to keep his mouth shut. It wouldn't do any good to explain that he'd lied about the reason he'd broken off their engagement. That he wasn't in Roger's pocket. That he'd given her up to protect her from Roger's threats. She wouldn't believe him anyway. Not unless he told her the whole story. And he could *never* tell her the whole story. "Stay away from my sister."

Britt's eyebrows arched in surprise. "Your sister? I hardly spoke to your sister."

"Stay away from her."

Her look shot daggers. "Kim is a possible witness. I have a right—an obligation—to speak to witnesses."

"If you need to question her, clear it through me."

"Why would you say that? Does Kim have something to hide?"

"Kimberly? Get real." Now she was making him angry. "Kimberly is getting married. I don't want you ruining her happiness with your unfounded attack on Grant."

She studied him for a moment over her coffee cup rim, then took a sip. And another. She actually appeared to enjoy the brew. The woman had cast-iron tastebuds.

Finally, she lowered the cup and glared at him. "There is nothing unfounded about this case."

Jack shook his head. Who did she think she was fooling? "We both know this case is more about revenge than evidence."

She clenched the cup, her long fingers wrapping clear around its circumference. "Go to hell, Jack. I didn't carry a torch for you five minutes, let alone five years."

He only wished that were true. But even now when she looked at him, the hurt and anger in her eyes throbbed as fresh and raw as the night he'd pulled her aside at their engagement party and declared all was over between them.

He stifled the answering pang in his chest. "This is between you and me. Leave the family out of it."

She crooked an eyebrow. "The family? You're sounding more like your father every day. I guess I shouldn't be surprised."

Jack gritted his teeth. He wouldn't let her get to him. He'd come here to force Britt to back off, and he wouldn't leave until he'd succeeded. "What do you hope to prove? I said I was sorry five years ago. Do you want me to grovel for your forgiveness?"

She narrowed her eyes to blue slits. "Believe it or not, Jack, this has nothing to do with you. It's about finding Tangi's murderer."

"Or assuaging your own guilt because you couldn't change Tangi, and you could never accept her the way she was."

Britt flinched as if he'd hit her.

Regret clubbed him square in the chest. Why did he have to say that? Why did she have to look at him like that? And why the hell couldn't he keep his personal feelings for her in the past? "I'm sorry, that was out of line."

Cold contempt replaced the hurt in her eyes. "Yes, it was. We were discussing Grant. And if I find Grant killed Tangi, I'm going to make sure he pays."

"And how do you plan to accomplish that?"

Britt smoothed a hand over her hair. She used to wear it loose, rippling to her shoulders like pale gold silk. He'd loved running his fingers through it, loved how it draped around his face like a gossamer curtain when she leaned over him.

Now she bound it like an uptight schoolmarm. She frowned, completing the look. "You don't expect me to outline my strategy, do you?"

"You don't have a strategy."

She glanced down at her uneaten bagel. "You're wrong."

No, he was right. Jack had been in too many courtrooms and dealt with too many district attorneys to miss the signs. Besides, he knew Britt. She was a master of the direct statement, the pure, unvarnished truth. And as a result, she couldn't lie worth a damn. "You haven't charged Grant because you don't have a case against him. Face it, Britt, he didn't do it."

Britt looked him dead in the eye, jutting her chin forward in that stubborn way of hers. "I'm still in the investigation stage. I'm building a case."

"What are you building it with? Wishful thinking? You don't have anything on Grant."

She took another sip of that godawful coffee. "Tangi was pregnant with Grant's baby."

The baby. Damn Grant. He didn't know the meaning of the word discretion. Not to mention responsibility, honesty, and a dictionary full of similar terms. Why on earth couldn't he keep it in his pants? Or, at the very least, use protection. "You have no evidence proving the baby was Grant's."

Britt sighed. "I will once I test Grant's blood for a DNA match with Tangi's baby."

"You'll need a court order for that. I'll see you never get it."

"Listen, Jack. We both know the baby was Grant's."

Jack shrugged. Probably. But he wouldn't admit it out loud. Not to her.

Britt smiled. "And according to Tia, Tangi was blackmailing Grant. That sounds like motive to me."

Shock ricocheted through Jack's mind. He tried to hide the surprise that must be written all over his face. Blackmail. So that was what Grant was hiding. Outrage pounded in his head like a bass drum. Neither Grant nor Tia had breathed a word of this to him in all the hours he'd spent grilling them. But in one short meeting, Tia had managed to tell Britt. He could strangle both Grant and Tia. Didn't they know how serious this situation could become? Hadn't he drilled that message into their thick heads by now?

"They didn't tell you, huh? Sorry I had to be the one to break the news." Judging from her grin, she wasn't at all sorry.

Jack drained his coffee cup. He needed time to regroup. Time to think. The café had grown quiet, the lunch crowd having returned to work. Somehow, the quiet made thinking harder. He could hear Britt's gentle breathing, feel her blue eyes studying him. How the hell was he going to dig himself out of this mess?

Time to throw himself on the mercy of the court. "Kimberly's wedding is very important to her. Can't you leave her alone until after her wedding?"

Britt bit into her bagel and chewed slowly. She followed with a sip of coffee. Raising her gaze to meet his, she opened her mouth to speak.

Jack held up his hand. He wasn't finished yet. "And don't get any ideas about arresting Grant. Even if you manage to dig up something that passes for evidence, I want you to hold off charging him until after the wedding."

She smiled and returned her attention to her lunch.

Jack tensed. He could see the gears turning in that mind of hers, feel her weighing her options.

She plunked her cup on the table with a decisive thud. "Deal."

If Jack had been chewing gum, he'd have swallowed it. Instead, he nodded as calmly as possible and waited for her conditions.

She crossed her knees, her trench coat falling open to reveal a navy blue skirt and those long, delicious legs. "I'll leave Kim alone and wait until after her wedding to arrest Grant on one condition."

Jack braced himself. He had the feeling he would hate this proviso. "What?"

"I'll wait until after Kim's wedding, provided you let me interview Grant."

Jack's every lawyerly impulse cringed. "You mean interrogate him."

She shrugged. "Do you want me to back off or not?"

His pulse drummed in his ears. He balled his hands into fists beneath the table. He'd persuaded her to back off, all right. But was her price too high?

Britt turned her attention back to her bagel and coffee, providing him time to think about her proposition.

As Grant's lawyer, Jack had a duty to protect him. Normally, he prevented his clients from talking to the authorities at all costs. But this wasn't a normal situation. He wasn't about to make Kimberly pay for Grant's weakness.

Jack drummed his fingers on his thigh. If he could control the circumstances of the interview, maybe he could protect everybody involved. He cleared his throat. "I'll bring the matter to Grant, provided I choose the time and place, the meeting is strictly off the record, and only you, Grant, and I are present."

Britt shook her head. "The detective working the case has to be present."

"So he can testify about the meeting in court? Nice try, Britt." Jack pushed back from the table, the chair legs screeching across the worn linoleum tile. He stood. He couldn't allow Britt a witness to the meeting. If she didn't agree to come alone, he couldn't justify the risk. As much as he wanted to protect the rest of his family, he couldn't just throw Grant to the wolves. He shrugged into his own trench coat.

Britt looked up at him, watching him, an ardent glow in her eyes. A glow he knew so well—and missed so much. "Have it your way. I can clear a few hours tomorrow afternoon."

Jack shook his head. Tomorrow was too soon. He needed time to go over Grant's story again, detail by detail. He couldn't afford any more surprises like Tangi's alleged blackmail. Three days of grilling Grant and Tia should do it. "Friday."

Britt's turn to shake her head. "Tangi's funeral is Friday."

Tangi's funeral. Jack knew how close Britt and

Tangi were, and for a moment, sympathy stirred inside him.

He deflected it. In this case, Britt was his adversary. He had to seize every advantage he could. Use everything he knew about her as a weapon against her. She'd be upset after watching her friend buried. She'd be distracted.

Perfect.

"Friday. After the funeral." He walked out before she could protest, the café's dull chime ringing in his ears.

Chapter Four

Britt strode past the black hearse and set off across the cemetery lawn. Dodging headstones and manicured shrubbery, she forced herself to focus straight ahead. She must keep her clamoring emotions under control. She hadn't set foot in a cemetery since her mother's burial, and she'd give anything to not have to step in one now.

Everything about her mother's death had been so unfair. Lung cancer attacked people who smoked, and Britt's mother had never taken a drag off a cigarette in her life. But Britt could have dealt with the unfairness of the disease. It was the secrecy that still made her muscles knot in anger. The secrecy that made her want to shake her mother and scream.

With each footfall, her legs grew heavier and the pain in her heart sharpened. Resentment built inside her until her head throbbed. She'd been cheated. First of her mother. And now of Tangi. At least she could make someone pay for Tangi's death.

A gust of wind battered her face and threatened to rip her black umbrella from her grasp. She turned up her collar and gripped the handle tighter. All traces of morning sun absent, the overcast sky couldn't decide whether to drizzle or sleet. Either way, the weather added up to miserable. Perfect day for a funeral.

Britt's heels sank into the not-yet-frozen sod. Shifting her weight to her toes, she broke into a tiptoed scamper. At least she'd had the foresight to drop her dad at the house before making her trek to the cemetery. Negotiating the soggy grass with his wheelchair would have been impossible. Although that prospect didn't bother her as much as the sadness that lined his face. He'd barely made it through the church service. And although Dad loved Tangi like a second daughter, Britt had a feeling the tears that glistened in his eyes were more for Britt's mother.

No, it was better that he skipped the burial. The memories would have been too much for him.

How she had survived the church service with dry eyes, she didn't know. Maybe her anger had helped her through. It had never been far below the surface since her mother's death. Or maybe she had no tears left. She'd know soon enough.

She hoped like hell she could get through the burial without falling apart. She needed to stay composed so she'd be sharp for her meeting with the Alcott boys.

Damn Jack. She'd spent the last three days cursing him, and it still felt good. Why did she let him dictate the terms of her meeting with Grant? He'd set the meeting after Tangi's funeral because he knew she'd be so upset she couldn't keep her mind on the interview.

Well, guess again, Jack.

Cresting the hill, she sucked in a breath. Under a white canopy, a fresh gash cut into the hillside like an open wound. A pile of wet earth loomed nearby, covered with a tarp as if someone had tried to mask the abomination. A cold steel frame straddled the grave, a plain, brown casket resting on top.

Britt's heart tightened in her chest. Tangi's mother had selected a brown casket. Anyone who knew Tangi would have chosen red with brass accents, or burnished gold. Tangi hated brown.

Most likely, Tangi's mother didn't know what she liked. Most likely, she didn't care.

At least Tangi's favorite purple orchids hid most of the casket. The flowers had cost Britt a pretty penny, but they were worth it. Their delicate, exotic blooms were as beautiful and special as Tangi. Britt swallowed a surge of tears. Somehow she had to get through this.

She forced herself to take in the scene. When she spotted the elaborate arrangement of white roses at the foot of the casket, her skin prickled with hostility. The roses had been delivered to the church anonymously, but Britt knew who had sent them. All the Alcotts had a similar flashy style. If the roses hadn't been the only other flowers at the funeral, she would have thrown them into the trash.

Stopping a hundred feet from the small group of umbrellas huddled around the minister, Britt struggled to breathe. The light turnout at the church had dwindled to only six mourners. Her stomach churned. She longed to join them, take comfort from other people who knew Tangi and mourned her death. But something prevented her from taking the last few steps to the grave site. If she approached the grave, if she peered into the hole where Tangi's body would be lowered, Britt would fall apart for sure.

One of the group turned away from the minister and ambled across the lawn in her direction. Mylinski carried no umbrella, drizzle beading on his bald head like sweat. Reaching her, he draped an arm over her shoulders, his version of a hug. "How you holding up?"

Good question. She swallowed the lump in her throat and hoped her voice would function. "So far, so good."

He clattered a piece of sour apple candy against his teeth with his tongue. "Good. I take it Cassidy made it to the funeral service?"

"In all his glory."

Mylinski smiled gently. "Sorry I missed the service. I was at the hospital."

Britt nodded. After a lengthy search, Mylinski had found Tangi's mother in the hospital suffering from liver disease. When he'd told Darlene Rowe of her daughter's death, she'd shrugged and complained about lousy hospital food. "How's Darlene doing?"

"Didn't see her. They released her two days ago."

The damp wind cut Britt to the bone. Tangi's own mother hadn't bothered to show up at the funeral. Figures. Tangi hadn't mattered to Darlene when she was alive. Why would she matter now?

Mylinski cleared his throat. "I learned something else. Something real interesting."

"I'm all ears."

Mylinski reached into his pocket and pulled out one more piece in his endless stream of Jolly Ranchers candy. "I hear through the grapevine that Tangi paid off some gambling debts for her mother. Paid cash for the whole amount."

Britt pulled her coat more tightly around her.

Where would Tangi get the money to pay her mother's gambling debts? She never saved money. She went through the green stuff like she was running out of time. She *had* run out of time. Britt braced herself. "How much?"

"Twenty thousand, give or take."

Britt frowned. Disappointment settled on her heart like a shroud. Tia's accusations played through her mind. Blackmail. It was the only way Tangi could get her hands on that kind of money. She didn't want to believe Tangi capable of such a crime, but she had to face the truth. "I might know where she got that kind of money."

Mylinski raised his eyebrows. "Really? You heard about the loan shark?"

"A loan shark?" She scoured his eyes, searching for answers. What was he talking about? She hadn't heard anything about a loan shark, not from Tangi, not from anyone. "Where does a loan shark fit into this?"

"Rumor has it, Tangi borrowed the bucks from a small-time loan shark by the name of Marcus Spinnetti."

Shock zigged through her. "Where did you hear this?"

Mylinski shrugged. "Same guy who told me about the gambling debts. Believe me, he's a good source."

Britt clutched the handle of her umbrella. Tangi was in deeper trouble than Britt had ever dreamed. If she'd needed money, why hadn't she come to Britt? Why hadn't she told Britt how desperate she was?

Heartache deluged her, as cold and dank as the drizzle droning on her umbrella. Grant's money. Tangi must have planned to use the money she was bilking from Grant to pay off the loan shark. Britt struggled to catch her breath, to calm her raging emotions. She'd ask Grant about the blackmail. She'd find the truth one way or another.

She opened her mouth, then closed it. She hadn't mentioned her upcoming meeting with Grant to Mylinski. The detective's speech about rushing to judgement still echoed in her ears. Better to have evidence when she presented her theory to Mylinski this time. "How do you think this loan shark fits in?"

"The way I see it, Spinnetti wants his money, like yesterday. He roughs her up to make a point and goes too far. Covers up the murder by staging the car accident."

She nodded. His theory made perfect sense. If Mylinski was right, she wouldn't have to deal with Jack or the Alcott family again. His theory would solve all her problems. Then why didn't it feel right? "What else did you find?"

"Fingerprints. We've come up with two sets of unidentified fingerprints at the scene. We ran a search for Spinnetti's prints in the previous offender files, but came up empty. We're still looking."

Strange. Usually someone in Spinnetti's business had a rap sheet the length of a short novel. Once arrested, Spinnetti's fingerprints would have been entered into the computer files. "What do you plan to do now?"

"Find Spinnetti."

"I want to be there when you interrogate him."

Mylinski smiled and winked. "You'll be the first person I call."

Above the whistling wind, Britt could hear the minister incant his final blessing. He scattered a handful of dirt over the head of the casket. After bowing their heads one last time, the handful of mourners shuffled off in the direction of their cars. The minister followed, and Tangi's casket was alone.

Britt's lower lip trembled. She caught it between her teeth. Soon Tangi would be lowered into the grave. Her headstone would join the rows of marble stretching across the brown-green hill.

Mylinski reached for her hand and gave it a brief squeeze. "You go say your goodbyes. We'll go over the rest back at your office." He ambled off after the others, leaving her alone. He had nearly reached his brown sedan before Britt found the strength to move.

Clutching her umbrella in both hands, she strayed closer to the casket. Thoughts of her mother, of Tangi, of their good intentions and tragic lies swirled in her mind. Denied tears burned her sinuses. Sobs caught in her throat, nearly choking her. She wouldn't cry. She couldn't cry. Unable to look at the casket any longer, she closed her eyes.

She came to say goodbye to her friend. To tell Tangi one last time that she loved her. To promise she'd never forget her. She opened her mouth to speak, but her vocal cords refused to function.

She couldn't say goodbye.

Bowing her head, she let the umbrella fall from her grasp. Despair choked her. Unchecked tears streamed down her cheeks.

"Britt." Through her sobs, she heard a familiar voice.

"Jack." A tremor started in her heart and spread through her body, nearly knocking her to her knees. She spun to face him. Clawing through swirling grief and anger, she struggled to regain control. "What are you doing here?"

Raindrops sparkled in his hair like stars in a dark sky. A black trench coat cloaked his broad shoulders, glistening with diamonds of moisture. Damn him. Any mortal would be soaked and bedraggled in this drizzle. Only Jack Alcott could stand in the rain with no umbrella and look as composed as a judge on the bench. "It wasn't my idea to come."

Conscious of her drenched hair, melted makeup, and the tears coursing down her cheeks and collecting under her chin, she focused on the ground between them. Of all people to witness her breakdown, why did it have to be Jack? "Leave me alone. I want to be alone."

He raised his hand to her chin and tilted her head back, forcing her to look at him. His eyes latched on to hers, their smoky brown depths mesmerizing her like the hypnotic stare of a cobra.

The strength of his fingers and his masculine scent stirred wisps of memories deep inside her. Memories of laughter and long conversations. Memories of silence more intimate than words. A shudder rippled across her skin. Damn Jack. She didn't want to remember. Not after five years. Not ever.

She tossed her head, tearing away from his touch. "Our meeting is scheduled for eleven-thirty. I hoped I wouldn't have to see you until then."

He shrugged and said nothing.

She gritted her teeth, frustration unleashing a rush of hot blood to her cheeks. "What *are* you doing here?"

He stared at her a moment, then nodded toward Tangi's grave.

Heart lurching, Britt spun around.

Grant stood at the top of the casket. Head bowed, he clutched one of the white roses in his fist. He wore no coat, and his hair and suit jacket were dark with beaded drizzle.

She swallowed the anger that rose like bile in her throat. "Why did you bring *him* here?"

"Take it easy, Britt." Jack grasped her elbow.

She balled her trembling hands into fists. The spectacle of Tangi's murderer standing over her grave was almost more than she could take. "He has no right."

Jack's grip tightened, his fingers digging into her arm. "Hold on a minute. Have you ever considered that he may be grieving for Tangi, too?"

The idea nauseated her. If Grant had killed Tangi, she doubted he was in mourning. "Get him away from her."

Jack grabbed her other arm, spinning her around to face him. "Let Grant have his time. If you're wrong and Grant didn't kill Tangi, he deserves the chance to say goodbye."

Britt hesitated. Struggling to sort through the jumble of anguish and rage shaking her from the inside out, she drew herself to her full height and set her chin. She'd agree to almost anything if Jack would just take his hands off her and quit looking at her as if he cared how she felt. "Fine. If Grant's goodbye is so important to you, I'll give him two minutes. Now take your hands off me."

He did what she asked.

Free, she spun back to Grant in time to see him place the white rose on Tangi's casket and swipe his eyes with a fist. She remembered his reaction to the news of Tangi's death. He'd nearly collapsed in her office. And now this.

What did it mean? She simply didn't know. It didn't matter anyway. If Grant was indeed innocent, the evidence would prove it. She could walk away and never deal with Jack and his family again.

But if he was guilty, she would find a way to forget the past, forget her feelings for Jack. After all, she had a job to do. A promise to keep. And no one would get in her way. Not even Jackson Alcott.

Chapter Five

Draping her coat over her briefcase, Britt slid into the secluded booth and sized up Grant on the other side of the table. With the exception of his red-rimmed eyes, he looked more like a Congressman politicking at a business lunch than a suspect about to be questioned by an assistant district attorney.

Jack slid into the booth next to her. The sleeve of his suit coat brushed hers. His designer-clad thigh rubbed against her gray skirt.

She scooted close to the cool window, but still couldn't escape the masculine scents of leather and musk, and the hot pulse of his body heat. Something stirred deep within her. The spark of a fire she wanted to extinguish.

She glanced around the restaurant, anywhere but at him. Wood and brass, fluted white linen napkins and crystal wine glasses, fresh flowers and soft jazz. Leave it to a snake like Jack to choose this place for their meeting. She'd dined here dozens of times, but never had the restaurant seemed so romantic. But then, she had never been here with Jack.

Memories of intimate conversations over glasses of Pinot Noir hovered in her mind. Trying new restaurants used to be a sport with them. An adventure. When she and Jack had been together, all of life had sparkled.

But that was over now.

She had to focus. She was here to talk to Grant, not Jack. She couldn't shake the sense that Grant's alibi was not what it seemed. Her confrontation with Tia in the bridal boutique only strengthened her suspicions. Grant and Tia weren't telling the truth about the night Tangi died. And Britt wanted the truth. "Shall we get started?"

Jack held up a hand, summoning a waiter. "First, we order."

The waiter, a pimply-faced boy probably working his way through college, peered at Britt.

"Nothing for me." She refused to pretend this gathering was a pleasant lunch date. She hated stall tactics. And she hated diversions.

Jack leaned toward her as if he were whispering an endearment in her ear. "You have to eat lunch, Britt. Order something. My treat."

His breath fanned her cheek, sending warmth fluttering up her spine. She pushed the ghosts of memory out of her mind. Warm whispers and a free lunch would not earn him points with her. "Coffee, black."

"I'll have a glass of Pinot Noir."

She scowled at him. Was he ordering Pinot Noir just to needle her, or was it just another wine to him now?

Jack nodded to the waiter, his expression matter-of-fact. No glance in her direction, no sly smile.

An ache settled in her chest. An ache she had no business feeling after five long years. He didn't remember. He'd purged those memories from his mind as effectively as he'd purged her from his life.

He turned to Grant. "Do you want a soda or something?"

"Chivas on the rocks. Make it a double."

Jack's turn to scowl. Apparently Grant wasn't falling into line either. "I thought you had a fund-raiser to attend."

Grant slumped back in the booth. Face pale and eyes rimmed with red, he looked like a man who could *use* a double scotch. "Kyle's filling in for me. He jumped at the chance to play politician for an afternoon."

Although tempered by understanding, the scowl didn't fade from Jack's face. Clearly, he worried about his brother. He'd never respected Grant, and he'd even disliked him at times. But Britt knew Jack had always cared about his brother, always protected him.

And Jack's worry and caring were the last things she wanted to acknowledge. She glanced out the window, looking to focus on anything but Jack. The federal courthouse stood across the street in all its garish glory. Purple curves, red pillars, and a red neon sculpture resembling a Slinky toy hanging from the ceiling, the structure did little to inspire confidence in the justice system.

The system aside, Britt had confidence in herself. She wasn't about to let old feelings for Jack interfere with Tangi's case. She needed to learn the truth about the night Tangi died and find out what Grant and Tia were hiding.

The waiter returned with Grant's drink, Britt's coffee, and Jack's wine and then left them alone.

Britt's heartbeat picked up its pace and nervous energy fluttered like butterflies against her stomach walls. Time to begin. "When did Tangi tell you she was pregnant with your baby?"

Grant peered at her over the rim of his scotch.

Jack held his glass aloft as if studying the wine's ruby color in the muted sunlight filtering through the window. "Nice try, Britt. Grant hasn't stipulated that the baby was his. Therefore, it isn't possible for him to answer the question as asked."

Annoyance with herself hummed in her ears. Of course Jack was too smart to let Grant answer that question. She wasn't up against some amateur here.

She reached for her cup of coffee. Sipping, she swallowed her frustration. She'd played games with defense attorneys before, but Jack was the best. There would be no fooling him. She'd have to rely on straightforward, point-blank questions to uncover the truth. "How long did you have an affair with Tangi?"

"I loved Tangi." Grant cleared his throat, a catch of emotion in his rough-edged voice. "We've been together off and on since I met her at the country club the night of your engagement party."

Britt nodded. After Britt's initial disapproval, Tangi had avoided speaking of her affair with Grant. But Britt suspected they'd been involved all along. When Tangi confided in Britt about her pregnancy shortly before her death, she'd said the news would shatter the Alcotts' country-club world. "Did you know Tangi was pregnant?"

"Yes." Grant swirled the liquid and ice in his tumbler.

"And when did she tell you this?"

"About two weeks ago."

"When did she tell you the baby was yours?"

Jack's hands shot up. If he'd had a gavel, he would have pounded it. "Grant has answered the question to the best of his ability. Move on."

"Certainly, Your Honor." Britt let the sarcasm ooze from her voice. She knew Jack would object to the question. The last thing he wanted was for Grant to admit he was the father of Tangi's baby. She turned back to Grant. "Was Tangi blackmailing you?"

Grant swirled his glass faster, the ice cubes jingling against the crystal like an unanswered doorbell.

Britt leaned forward, careful not to brush against Jack. One more try. "Was Tangi blackmailing you?"

Shaking his head, Grant plunked the tumbler on the table. "She didn't blackmail me. She just asked me for money. You know, to help her out. She never threatened me with anything."

Jack's head snapped around. He glared at his brother as if contemplating punching him in the mouth to shut him up.

Britt reclined in the bench, trying to digest this new information. She focused on Grant, struggling to see through his polished political veneer. "How much money did you give her?"

Grant didn't even blink. "I didn't get the chance to give her anything. She asked me for the money two days before she died."

"Tia seems to think Tangi blackmailed you. Why is that?"

Jack tensed beside her.

Grant gulped scotch, shaking his head while he guzzled the glass of amber liquid. When he set the glass down and opened his mouth to answer, the sweet fumes of his breath made her stomach roll.

"Ever since she started her housing crusade, Tia practically lives at the bank. She wanted to know why I withdrew that much cash. What was I supposed to tell her?"

Britt's skin prickled at the helpless tone in his voice. Grant the victim. Just a poor helpless guy trying to protect the women in his life. Right. It probably never occurred to him to tell the truth. "So Tia was mistaken. Tangi wasn't blackmailing you."

"No. Tangi needed the money. I tried to get it for her." He splayed his hands in front of him palms up as if begging for her understanding. "Like I said, I loved her. I couldn't explain that to Tia."

Britt scoffed. "I guess not."

Grant gripped his scotch in both hands. "I loved her," he repeated under his breath.

Sure he did. That's why he painted her as a heartless bitch capable of blackmail in order to save his own skin. Call her a romantic, but she expected a little more from a man in love. "Why did she need money?"

Jack reached for his glass of wine, his arm brushing Britt's shoulder. "How would Grant know Tangi's reasons?"

Heat surged through her body at his touch. She pressed back against the cool windowsill and glared at him. "I would ask before handing someone twenty thousand dollars, wouldn't you?"

Jack shook his head and met her eyes. "When you're in love with someone, you trust them."

Britt narrowed her eyes and gritted her teeth. A lecture in trust from Jack Alcott? Give her a break. Her best defense was to ignore him. He and his Pinot Noir could take a flying leap. She focused on his brother. "Why did Tangi need the money?" she repeated.

Grant glanced from Jack to her.

Jack waved a hand in the air. "Go ahead and answer."

Grant hunched over his glass, staring at the last dregs of amber liquid inside. "Tangi had borrowed some money to pay her mother's gambling debts. She wanted to pay back the loan."

She arched an eyebrow. Did he know about Mylinski's loan shark? "So you gave her money and lied to your wife so Tangi could pay back a loan? That seems a bit radical to me. Most banks accept payments over time. Why couldn't she just pay a little each month?"

Grant shifted in his seat, as if growing uncomfortable with her questions.

Tough luck. She had a lot more lethal questions than this in the firing chamber. "Why the hurry to pay back the loan?"

"Tangi didn't go to a bank. She dealt with a loan shark. He wanted his money."

Her heart pumped with enthusiasm. Maybe Mylinski was onto something. Maybe Grant hadn't murdered Tangi. Maybe this loan shark was responsible all along.

Jack stirred next to her, his leg inches from hers, his closeness overpowering her senses.

She knew one thing, the sooner she got away from Jack, the safer she'd feel. "What do you know about this loan shark?"

Grant tapped his index finger on the table, his movement jerky, nervous. "He's the one you should be looking for. He's the son-of-a-bitch who killed Tangi.''

''Does he have a name?''

Grant shook his head.

Jack leaned forward in the booth. ''Think, Grant. She must have told you his name.''

Britt almost laughed. A moment ago Jack wanted his brother to keep quiet. Now his eagerness for Grant to point the finger at another suspect had him drooling.

A furrow grooved into Grant's brow. ''Something Italian. Spinnotta, Spinnozzi…''

''Spinnetti?'' Britt offered.

''That's it.''

Jack turned to Britt. ''There's your prime suspect. Now, Grant has to leave. If you want to take me up on my offer of lunch, you're more than welcome.''

Not so fast. She still didn't know why Grant and Tia's alibis seemed so fishy, and Grant wasn't leaving until she figured out the reason. ''What about Tia? Did she know about the baby?''

Grant's cheeks reddened. Whether caused by her question or the scotch, she couldn't tell.

But she'd find out. ''Well? Did she know about the baby or not?''

Jack coiled, ready to strike.

Grant's color deepened. His eyes darted around the dining room as if searching for a way out. ''Tia didn't know anything,'' he protested, his words a little too loud, a little too panicked.

Britt tensed. Maybe she had been wrong. Maybe Tia wasn't covering for Grant. Maybe Grant was covering for Tia. ''If I remember correctly, you and Tia have been trying to have a baby for the last—what is it now? Seven years? I'll bet she was upset to learn you fathered another woman's child.''

Jack shot her a stormy look. ''That's enough. You're out of line, Britt.''

''Maybe she was upset enough to kill.''

''You can't be serious,'' Grant bellowed, bulling his way out of the booth. ''Tia didn't kill Tangi.''

''This interview is over.'' Jack motioned his brother toward the exit. ''Get out of here, Grant. Now.''

''I was with Tia all night,'' Grant shot over his shoulder. ''At the Monona Terrace Convention Center and then at home.'' He slammed from the restaurant, almost knocking over a waiter's tray of salads in the process.

Britt watched him leave, an uneasy feeling stealing over her skin. ''At the Monona Terrace Convention Center and then at home,'' she repeated. ''Tia said the same thing, word for word, in her witness statement to the police *and* when I talked to her at the bridal boutique. Doesn't that strike you as strange?''

Jack angled his body to face her. Even the cloud-filtered light from the window couldn't soften the stark, powerful lines of his face. A face that could show so much passion. And so much tenderness. ''First Grant and now Tia? Why are you so hell-bent on accusing a member of the family? Why are you ignoring this Spinnetti character?''

''I'm not accusing, I'm investigating. I'll only accuse Grant or Tia if the evidence says they're guilty.''

''I think you're trying to manufacture something to be suspicious about. You have a suspect. The loan shark wanted his money. Tangi couldn't pay.''

She considered his argument. She wanted to believe the truth could be that simple, that logical. Just as in the past, she had wanted to believe every word Jack said.

But she couldn't believe Jack. She couldn't trust him. She'd learned that lesson five years ago. And she wasn't about to make that mistake again. "If Spinnetti killed her, how would he get his money?"

"It was her mother's debt. Maybe he figured Tangi's death would send her mother a message."

Britt shook her head. "Without Tangi, Darlene could never come up with twenty thousand dollars."

"Well, I happen to think a loan shark is more likely to commit murder than a U.S. Congressman."

"A lot of people would differ with that opinion."

Jack flashed her a sarcastic smile. "Cute."

Tilting her head, she returned the smile, then fixed him with a sincere stare. She hadn't come here to trade barbs with Jack. She wanted information. "Seriously, Jack. Something isn't right about Grant and Tia's story. I just want to know what it is."

"Even if I knew the answer, I couldn't tell you, Britt. You know that." He smiled gently. A shard of sunlight pierced the overcast sky, sparking off the mahogany highlights in his dark hair.

Britt's throat closed. God, he was an attractive man. Memories swamped her, threatening to drag her under. The warmth of his skin against hers. The gruffness of his laugh in the morning. The flavor of his kiss.

Her heart lurched in her chest. She looked away. She couldn't be near him any longer. Not in this romantic place. Not with him sitting so close, smiling at her like the Jack from her memories. Truth or no truth, she had to get out of here. She had to get away from him. "I have to go."

JACK WATCHED BRITT scamper between the tables and out the restaurant's door, her black satin hair ribbon waving goodbye with each stride. A warm calm settled inside him. Amazing. For a moment there, they'd connected. Shared ideas. No games. No anger.

For a moment, just a moment, she'd looked at him with the same openness, the same honesty, the same trust that she used to. Trust he had destroyed when he broke off their engagement.

He drew himself up and tore his gaze from the restaurant door. He couldn't let the past sidetrack him. He needed to keep his mind on protecting Grant.

Uneasiness settled into his muscles. Grant and Tia were still lying about something. Britt had noticed the same unusual repetition in their story that he had. But of course, her well-honed mind had never missed a trick in the past, why would she start missing things now?

But it was a suspicion, a hunch. She still had no evidence that either Grant or Tia killed Tangi, no matter what spin she wanted to give the repetition in their story.

A shot of acid gurgled into his stomach. He'd gotten so wrapped up in their momentary connection, he hadn't even attempted to point out her lack of evidence. He had to make that clear to her. Why had he let her leave before he'd made that clear?

He threw some cash on the table, and then strode from the restaurant. He'd catch up with her before she reached her car. His pulse picked up its tempo at the thought of talking with her again, connecting with her again. He shook his head. Was he losing his mind? He didn't want a connection. He wanted to set her straight. This time he wouldn't let old feelings sidetrack him. He'd remind her that her hunch meant nothing—proved nothing.

Humidity hung in the outside air like a shroud, cold and dank. At least it had stopped raining. Still, the street was quiet for the noon hour.

Jack surveyed the corner. The sound of high heels tapping against pavement echoed off the parking ramp across the street. There she was, hurrying toward the ramp, her coat flapping in the light breeze.

"Britt."

She didn't turn around. In fact, if he wasn't mistaken, her pace quickened.

"Britt, wait. I need to talk to you."

The door to the stairwell closed behind her with a thud.

Apparently, she was finished talking. Too bad he wasn't. He had to set this matter straight before it snowballed. He jogged across the street, his muscles reveling in the exercise. A dozen strides, and he entered the stairwell.

Footsteps sounded on the flight above.

He followed the sound, taking the steps two at a time.

A door creaked open and slammed shut, echoing through the stairwell.

Reaching the door to level C, he threw it open and followed her into the guts of the parking ramp. By the time he spotted her, she'd almost reached her car.

"Britt."

She marched toward the blue Corsica, ignoring his call.

Anger rifled his composure. She couldn't just *ignore* him. She could tell him to get lost. She could spit in his face if she wanted, but she couldn't *ignore* him. He broke into a jog to catch her.

The squeal of rubber on concrete slashed through the ramp, echoing off the walls and floor. A black sedan whipped around the corner, the ramp's ceiling lights glinting off windows tinted the color of gun steel.

Britt was in the car's path. *God, no.*

The sedan accelerated. Tires screeched. The car shot straight for her.

''Britt!'' Jack bellowed. He lunged for her, lowering his shoulders.

She turned in the direction of the sound.

He hit her full force just as the car roared inches away.

She sprawled to the floor, and he landed on top of her, knocking the breath from his lungs.

Chapter Six

"Britt?" Jack stroked her cheek with unsteady fingers. "Britt, can you hear me?"

She turned her head to the side, breathing in coughing gasps.

Relief shuddered through him. She could move. She could breathe. "Britt, are you all right?"

"I'm fine," she answered in a brave voice. "Just fine."

She may be trying to sound convincing, but she failed miserably. "Can you stand?"

"I think so."

He embraced her, lifted her, and set her on her feet. He stole a glance at her hands and legs. The knees of her hose hung in tatters. Blood oozed from her raw palms.

She looked up at him, confusion in her vibrant blue eyes. "What was that?"

"That car tried to hit you. Didn't you see it?" Just saying the words out loud caused panic to spear though him. Pulling her to him, he pressed her head against his chest and brushed her forehead with his lips.

Her skin was soft, satin smooth. So fine. So delicate.

Anger whipped through him like wildfire fueled by dry wood and strong wind. The driver of the black sedan, whoever the hell he was, had accelerated coming off the curve. Britt had been right in the car's path when the driver hit the gas. No question, the driver had been gunning for her. He'd tried to kill her. And if Jack hadn't followed her to the parking ramp, hadn't pushed her out of the car's path, the murdering bastard would have succeeded.

Britt trembled under his touch.

He guided her out of the traffic path. Leaning her against the trunk of a parked car, he stepped back to take a long hard look. She stared into space with unseeing eyes. Tears streaked her face. Blood congealed on her raw hands.

God, she was beautiful. Her smooth pale skin, her parted lips, her strands of pale blond hair struggling to escape the imprisoning ribbon. She inspired an ache inside him so deep, it took his breath away.

He tightened his grip on her arms, forcing her to look straight at him. "Who would try to kill you?"

"Try to kill me?" Britt stared at him as if he'd lost his mind.

"This was no accident. That driver accelerated. He gunned for you."

She shook her head.

Damn it, she had to take this seriously. She had to protect herself. "Has anyone threatened you?"

She screwed up her forehead and glanced down at his hands on her arms.

Realizing how tightly he held her, he loosened his

grip, but he didn't let go. "Damn it, Britt, answer me. Has anyone threatened you?"

She met his gaze, her eyes gleaming like sapphires. "Not any more than usual."

Jack nodded. He'd heard the same from other assistant district attorneys. Death threats from punks went along with the job. They blamed society. They blamed the schools. They blamed the prosecuting attorney. Everyone but themselves. Fortunately, these death threats were almost always bunk. "Anyone who sounded serious?"

"They all sound serious. But they never are."

"This one was."

She shrugged and looked away from him. Her chin quivered, and her eyes still held a sunken, hollow stare. This had upset her more than she wanted to let on. Good. At least denial hadn't totally blinded her to the danger.

Her light scent pierced the stench of car exhaust and oil. He fought the urge to lean closer, to fill his lungs with her fragrance. An empty ache flogged his chest. Stroking her satin cheek, he turned her face toward him. "Did anyone know you were meeting us at the White Horse Inn?"

"No."

"You didn't tell your secretary, or write it in an appointment book?"

She squinted her eyes, searching her memory. "No."

Jack's muscles bunched in frustration. He wanted to pace. He wanted to move. He wanted to *do* something. The driver of the black sedan had been lying in wait. Had known where Britt would be. "Think. You must have told someone."

She considered for a moment. "No one. Even if I wrote it down or told my secretary, how would some punk I prosecuted learn about it?"

He paused. She had a point. "Could someone have followed you?"

"I didn't notice anyone."

He couldn't miss the tinge of doubt in her voice. He'd seen her anguish at the cemetery. She'd been an emotional wreck when she'd driven to the restaurant, in no shape to notice a black car in her rearview mirror.

"Maybe you didn't see him. Maybe he knew you'd be at Tangi's funeral. Maybe he followed you from the cemetery." He traced the line of her cheekbone with his fingertips. So soft, so vulnerable.

She threw up her arms, knocking his hand away from her cheek. "Some punk just out of prison isn't going to know about my friendship with Tangi."

"It's possible that—"

"Give it up, Jack. No one followed me. No one knew where I was. Except Grant, of course." Fight and fire burned in Britt's eyes, her vulnerability buried deep once again.

Fight and fire were all well and good, but they wouldn't keep her safe. Not if she refused to acknowledge that someone—and it certainly wasn't Grant—was trying to kill her. "I'll drive you to a doctor. You need someone to look at your hands and knees. Then we'll notify the police."

"I have rubbing alcohol and bandages at home. And I can notify the police when I get back to the office, which is where I should be right now." She whirled away from him and limped toward her little blue car. She unlocked the door. Once inside, she slammed the door behind her and pushed the lock.

Frustration seized his gut. He spun around and dashed for his own car. She might refuse to take this attempt on her life seriously, but he wouldn't make that mistake. With some maniac after her, he wasn't about to let her drive off alone. He could at least follow her to her destination.

He retrieved his Jag and caught up to Britt as she paid for her parking. He wanted to stop her car, drag her into his, and whisk her away to a place where the driver of the black car couldn't find her. A place where he could keep her safe.

He paid for his parking and joined the traffic on the street, keeping her car in sight.

The flavor of Pinot Noir lingered on his palate like a specter from the past. He'd enjoyed the wine in the past five years, but today in the restaurant its flavor had been sweeter, sharper, more robust. Like the memories it inspired.

Britt hadn't reacted when he'd ordered the wine. She probably didn't want to remember the bottles they'd shared when they'd been together.

But he couldn't stop himself from remembering.

He'd never been happier than the day she'd agreed to marry him. He'd taken her to scout sites for his Bonanza Boys' Ranch in northern Wisconsin, land thick with towering pines. In a quiet clearing under jagged rock faces, he'd popped the question.

The joy on her face had been his answer. And at that moment, he knew he'd do anything for this woman.

It had almost killed him to walk away, but he'd done so with her well-being foremost in his mind. As long as he stayed away, he knew she would have the career she had worked so hard for and the father who adored her. In time she would get over losing him.

But now someone had tried to kill her. His walking away couldn't spare her this time.

His heart wrenched and anger roared in his ears. If she refused to protect herself, he'd do it for her, damn it. He'd find the person trying to hurt her. He would make the bastard pay.

BRITT LIMPED up the sidewalk to her front door, aware of Jack's stare burning into her back. He wouldn't leave her alone, damn him. He'd followed her all the way home.

She dug through her purse. Hands aching, she fumbled with her jangling key chain. She couldn't wait to get inside the door and away from Jack. His tender touch and penetrating gaze was more than she could take.

As much as she loved him five years ago, she hated him now. She hated the soft caress of his fingers. She hated the way his musk-and-leather scent stirred her. But most of all, she hated her own longing to trust that the concern in his husky baritone was real. Or lasting.

She opened the door and lunged into the safety of her house, slamming the door behind her so hard, the windows rattled.

"Britt? What's wrong, hon?" Dad's worried voice hailed from the kitchen. Even without seeing her, he must have realized something was up.

Damn. She'd hoped that he'd already left for the big euchre tournament at the VFW tonight. No such luck. She peered down at her tattered panty hose, at her stinging hands, and then into the mirror hanging on the foyer's wall. Her flushed face stared back, tear tracks streaking her makeup like raindrops on a dirty windshield.

She glanced around the small entry hall, searching for an escape route. If her dad saw her in this kind of shape, he'd hit the panic button. He'd call in every favor his old colleagues in the police department owed him. He'd ask them to tail her every minute of every day. "I have a run in my hose. I have to change before going back to the office. Talk to you in a second."

She didn't get the chance to escape.

He rolled into the hall in his wheelchair, the overhead light catching the silver threading through his blond hair, his old Green Bay Packer henley stretched taut across his barrel chest. Eyes narrowing, he assessed her condition. His face showed little emotion. It never did. He rarely smiled or frowned. He rarely laughed or growled. Britt's mother used to say a Norwegian shell protected his tender heart. But even though his expression never changed, it was clear that right now his tender heart was concerned about her. "What happened?"

"I'm okay, Dad. Don't worry."

He reached for her, grasping her forearm, careful not to touch her raw hands. He didn't have to say a word for Britt to understand his demand. He wanted answers. Now.

She filled him in on the dry facts, the interview with Grant, the black car, and Jack's fortuitous tackle.

Darkness settled over her dad's face, a weight she hadn't seen for years. He shot her a look as if he suspected she'd left out half the story. "And? What else?"

She set her chin and kept her mouth shut. She couldn't tell him about the longing that assailed her when Jack held her in his arms. Nor about the old feelings and memories that rushed back when he'd brushed his lips to her forehead. She didn't want to admit these feelings to herself.

"I'm calling Neil Fitzroy. You're not working on Tangi's case any longer."

Britt stepped back. Just as she feared, her dad was overreacting. "The car almost running me down has nothing to do with Tangi's case."

"Are you sure about that? Do you think Roger Alcott is the type of man who'd sit around and wait for you to charge his boy with murder?"

"I'm sure this incident has nothing to do with Tangi's case. I've gotten dozens of death threats, you know that."

"And dozens of punks haven't made good on them."

"Exactly."

"And what has changed this week?"

She bit her bottom lip. The only thing different this week was her investigation of Tangi's death. But that still didn't mean the attempt on her life in the parking ramp was related. Any number of scenarios were more likely. Britt juggled a number of cases in any given week. And while Tangi's case was her only homicide, she also had a rape case and a violent assault on her schedule. Not to mention all of her past cases. "Your assumption is based on your hatred for the Alcotts. It has nothing to do with the evidence."

He clutched the arms of his wheelchair with such

force, his knuckles grew pale. "I don't need evidence to know my daughter is in danger, and those high and mighty Alcotts are to blame."

She set her chin. How could an intelligent man like her father have such an extreme case of tunnel vision? She couldn't give up the case. Why couldn't he understand that? She had to know who killed Tangi. She had to bring the murderer to justice. "I'm not giving up the case, Dad."

He scowled and crossed his arms over his chest.

She sighed. Arguing with her father never got her anywhere. Her mother had been right. The man was as stubborn as a tree stump with deep roots. But her mother always drew the line. Time for Britt to do exactly that. "I'm an adult. I have a job to do. Back off and let me do it."

No discernible emotion flickered in his eyes. Just the darkness, the weight. "If you insist on going ahead with this, at least you can promise me one thing."

She started toward her bedroom, then stopped and turned to listen. Her dad had every right to be concerned. She understood his fear for her. He'd seen her through the months, the years, following Jack's betrayal. He'd been her rock, her comfort, the only man she could trust. She didn't want to shut him out just because he cared about her. At least she could let him say his piece. "What?"

"Stay away from the Alcotts."

"You know I can't do that. Not if Grant is a strong suspect."

His blue eyes looked tired, old. "It's not Grant I'm most worried about. You're good at your job. I have no doubt you can handle Grant. Jack is another story."

Britt's stomach clenched. Her heart tossed and turned. Memories of Jack's lips brushing her forehead sent shivers rippling over her skin. Her dad had reason to worry. She was worried out of her mind. "I'll try. I promise I'll try."

The ring of the cordless phone jolted her. She rushed past her dad and into the kitchen to answer it. "Hello?"

"Britt? It's Al. Remember our friend the loan shark?"

"Marcus Spinnetti?"

"Right. We got him. Cassidy picked him up coming out of his girlfriend's house. He's cooling his heels in the interrogation room. Want to come down and say howdy?"

Britt drew in a deep breath and then exhaled. If Mylinski's hunch was right and she could prove Spinnetti killed Tangi, all her worries would be over. Not only would Tangi's murderer be behind bars, but Britt could keep her promise to her dad. She would never have to hear Jack's voice or feel his touch again. "I'll be there as soon as I can."

BRITT SLIPPED INTO the shoe-box-sized cubicle adjoining the interrogation room. Dan Cassidy leaned unmoving in the corner. Mylinski shot to his feet in front of the one-way window into the interrogation room, almost knocking over his chair. Both men gripped stained coffee mugs. Judging from Mylinski's sudden movement, he'd consumed more than enough of his high-octane brew.

The tight quarters reeked of strong coffee and

strong sweat. She wrinkled her nose and peered around Mylinski's shoulder and into the interrogation room, trying to get a glimpse of Spinnetti. Good thing she didn't have to stay in here. The smell made her eyes water.

Eyeing the bandages on her hands, Mylinski raised his eyebrows, but said nothing.

"I fell." Hopefully he'd accept that as an explanation. After her dad's reaction, she'd rather avoid telling Mylinski the story of her brush with death.

To her relief, he nodded. "Looks like I might owe you an apology."

"For what?"

"The lab identified one set of fingerprints in Tangi's apartment. Guess whose name came up on the computer?" Mylinski grinned like a game-show host, waiting for her answer.

She didn't have to ponder the question long. "Grant. Grant's fingerprints were in Tangi's apartment."

"Bingo. After they exhausted the criminal files, they checked out the government files like you suggested."

Britt nodded, considering this. All government employees had to be fingerprinted. When she'd started in the district attorney's office, she'd had to go through the ritual herself. As a lifelong politician, Grant had submitted to the same procedure.

But the lab technicians had no way of knowing if he'd left the prints in Tangi's apartment the night of her murder, or last Christmas. The evidence might be valuable in court, but fingerprints alone wouldn't be enough to convince a judge to issue a search warrant or arrest warrant. "I talked to Grant this noon. Among other things, he admitted his affair with Tangi. It's logical that his prints would be in her apartment."

Mylinski's grin faded. "Well, there's always the other prints."

Yes, the other prints. "Do you think they're Spinnetti's?"

Cassidy piped up from the corner. "You better believe it."

She barely glanced at Cassidy. His assurances didn't put her mind at ease. She knew she shouldn't be so hard on him. From all appearances, he'd done a good job persuading Spinnetti to come in for questioning. But, she'd given Cassidy the benefit of the doubt many times in the past, and every time he'd burned her.

She'd stick with Al Mylinski's judgement. "What do you think, Al? Could the prints belong to Spinnetti?"

He shrugged. "We hope."

Britt drew in a deep breath of foul air. No one hoped more than she did.

"Want to see our boy?" Mylinski shifted to the side so she could see through the one-way mirror into the adjoining interrogation room.

Sprawled in a chair behind the bolted-down steel table, Marcus Spinnetti read a battered copy of *Sports Illustrated*. Built squat like a bulldog, he had a complexion the texture of chewed rawhide and a nose as long and pointed as a Doberman's. The arms of his white T-shirt strained to fit around biceps the circumference of tree trunks, and bulging muscle reinforced what little neck he had.

Probably good for the loan sharking business, all

that muscle. One look at those arms, and a smart person would pay him any amount of interest he wanted.

A shiver of energy sent butterflies dancing in her stomach. The same excitement she felt every time she questioned a witness or stepped into the courtroom to argue a point of law. The thrill of battle. The hunger to win. The thirst for the truth.

She drew in a deep breath and nodded to Mylinski. "Shall we?"

Mylinski smiled, his blue eyes twinkling with the same eager glint she knew shone in hers. "You want to play the good cop or the bad cop?"

She returned his smile. "Go ahead. I know you like to be the heavy."

He winked and opened the door.

Cassidy moved to the center of the window. He would observe the questioning and be on hand if they needed him.

Spinnetti didn't bother to look up from his magazine when they stepped into the room.

"Hello, Mr. Spinnetti. I'm Assistant District Attorney Gerritsen, and this is Detective Mylinski."

He lowered his reading material and yawned, lips stretching back from yellowed teeth. His gaze crawled over Britt, resting on the swell of her breasts. "You can call me Marcus, baby."

She forced a smile. Better men than him had tried to intimidate her with leering looks. All of them had failed. If this was his best attempt, he might as well hang it up right now. "Would you like a cup of coffee, Marcus?"

His gaze didn't waver. "Sure, baby. I like it hot, with lots of cream."

Too bad she hadn't chosen the bad cop role. It would be fun to threaten a creep like Spinnetti.

Mylinski half sat on the corner of the table and rolled his eyes, biding his time. If she knew Al, he was itching to put the screws to this jerk. He'd enjoy it even more if, after their chat, he could lead Spinnetti out of the interrogation room in handcuffs.

A tap sounded on the door. Britt opened it and accepted the steaming mug of coffee Cassidy handed her. She set it on the table in front of Spinnetti. "I have a few questions to ask you, Marcus."

"Yeah? You want to sit on my lap while you ask?"

Britt maintained her icy smile. This guy was a piece of work. "I'm more comfortable standing, thanks. Are you acquainted with a woman named Tangi Rowe?"

"If she looks like you, I wish I was."

"Some of her personal papers indicate you loaned her a great deal of money. Twenty thousand dollars, to be exact." In reality, the police had searched every inch of Tangi's apartment and found no such thing. Britt's guess was based on the information gleaned from Mylinski's informant. But a well-placed bluff tended to loosen tongues. Maybe this one would loosen Spinnetti's.

The loan shark shrugged. "So I lent the lady some money. So what?"

"So you charged her fifty percent interest on that money."

He glowered. "Do her papers tell you that, too?"

"As a matter of fact, yes."

"I don't care what she wrote down, she's lying. Tell the bitch she's a damn liar."

Britt studied his averted eyes. If he read the papers

or watched the local news, he knew Tangi was dead. He probably intended his ignorant act to throw them off course. If he had nothing to hide, why wouldn't he admit he'd heard of her death? "I would tell her that, Marcus. But you see, she's dead."

He met Britt's gaze, his predicament dawning on him. "You think I killed her?"

"I didn't say that. We just want to ask you a few questions, that's all."

Spinnetti nodded and returned his beady gaze to her bustline.

Sometimes being a woman in this business paid off. Criminals often didn't see her as a threat. Consequently, she could get away with maneuvering that many of her male counterparts wouldn't dare try. Spinnetti's total lack of respect for women made him an easy target. "Tell me about your deal with Tangi Rowe."

Spinnetti leaned back in his chair, sprawling his beefy legs wide and hooking his thumbs in the band of his jeans. "She came to me wanting money. I gave it to her. End of story."

"And what did you do when she wasn't able to pay you back?"

"What are you talking about? I got my money."

Britt almost did a double take. "When did you get your money?"

"What difference does it make? I got it. That's all I care about."

Tangi paid him? Impossible. Grant said he'd never had the chance to give her the money. And if the money hadn't come from Grant or Tangi, where had it come from? Someone was lying.

Mylinski circled the table. He loomed over the seated Spinnetti like the Grand Inquisitor.

Spinnetti didn't seem to notice, his gaze still combing Britt's body, his back slumped, his legs sprawled.

Mylinski slammed his fist on the table, the steel vibrating with the force of the blow. "Listen, you worthless bastard. I know you were in the lady's apartment the night she was killed. I have fingerprints to prove it."

Spinnetti turned to him and sneered. "Nice try, but I ain't been fingerprinted. You can't prove any fingerprints are mine."

The pieces clicked into place in Britt's mind. So that was why the lab couldn't find a match in the fingerprint files. His prints had never been entered. Britt would have to arrest him to obtain his fingerprints, and she didn't have the evidence to do that.

Mylinski leaned over him, looking him in the eye, his nose inches from Spinnetti's. "When she couldn't pay, you beat her up, didn't you? Beat her up bad. Only problem was, you went too far. You thought she was dead, so you tried to cover up."

Spinnetti rolled his eyes and reached for the cup of coffee on the table. Swallowing the stiff brew, he made a face. "Cops always make the worst coffee. Now if that's all you got, I'm going." He shifted forward in his seat as if to stand up.

Mylinski seized the loan shark's muscled shoulders and pushed him against the chair's back. Coffee sloshed over the cup's rim and splashed on the tabletop. "You killed her, you worthless bastard. Didn't you?"

Unshaken, Spinnetti set the empty cup on a dry spot on the table. He shot Britt a look, like he'd rather be talking to her. "Look, I ain't stupid. You got nothing to tie me to that girl. If you did, you'd have arrested me already."

Britt's heart sank. He'd seen through their act. She should have known a creep like Spinnetti would have enough experience getting around the law to understand the way the system worked. He may not have been arrested before, but he was no choirboy.

She glanced down at the coffee mug on the table. There might be a way to gain the upper hand with the loan shark after all. If the other set of fingerprints at Tangi's apartment belonged to Spinnetti, all she needed was a sample of his prints for a match. It was her only shot at reaching the truth.

And maybe her only shot at getting Jack out of her life.

She reached across the table and picked up the mug, careful to touch as little of the surface as possible.

Spinnetti's gaze followed her. If he had any clue what she was doing, he showed no sign.

With her free hand, Britt motioned to the one-way mirror. "Cassidy, come in here. And bring an evidence bag."

Dan Cassidy did as she asked.

She placed the cup in the bag. "Take this straight to the lab. I want a comparison of the fingerprints on this cup with the unidentified prints found at Tangi's apartment."

Cassidy nodded and left, cradling the bag in his hands.

Mylinski backed away from Spinnetti and leaned his back against the beige wall, a grin spreading from one ear to the other.

Britt smiled down at the guarded expression on Spinnetti's face. "Those prints are going to match, aren't they Marcus?"

He folded his arms across his chest, his biceps straining the white cotton T-shirt.

Mylinski clouted him in the shoulder with the butt of his hand. "Answer the lady."

Spinnetti glowered. "I didn't kill her. I just wanted my money."

Mylinski straightened. "But you beat her up?"

He shook his head. "I went to see her, but I didn't touch her. She was fine when I left."

Mylinski closed in on the loan shark. "What about the money?"

"Said she didn't have it. I gave her two more days."

Britt frowned. His story wasn't even close to adding up. "Five minutes ago, you said you got your money."

He shrugged. "I did. But I didn't get it from her."

Britt's stomach balled into a hard knot. She stepped away from the wall and leaned over the table, eye-level with the loan shark. "Who gave you the money?"

Spinnetti yawned, stretching his arms above his head. Picking his teeth with a dirty fingernail, he stared at her breasts once again, his ugly mug distorting into a leer.

"If you were paid, you obviously would no longer have a motive for murder. But the only way we can check out your story is to know who paid you, Marcus. So which is it? Are you going to give us the name of the person who paid you, or am I going to have to ask Detective Mylinski here to arrest you when we get the fingerprint results?''

He raised his eyes to meet hers. The leer still twisted his face, but there was something in his eyes. Something she hadn't seen before. Fear. "Word on the street is that you like the good congressman for the babe's murder. But he ain't the one that paid me.''

Relief poured into her, loosening the knot in her stomach. Although she had no assurances that Spinnetti was telling the truth, she couldn't help feeling as if a burden had been lifted from her shoulders. Maybe Grant wasn't involved. Maybe she could get Jack out of her life after all. "I'm asking you one last time and then I'm going to call down to the lab. Who paid you the twenty thousand dollars that Tangi Rowe owed you?''

Spinnetti stared at her, taking his sweet time. Finally, he opened his mouth. "I got the money from the congressman's old man. Roger Alcott.''

Chapter Seven

Jack drove his Jag past the guest parking lot outside his lakeside condominium. A white Mercedes parked diagonally across two spaces. Kyle's car. Great. No doubt he was waiting in the lobby. Hell, if Kyle had gotten ahold of the spare key Jack had given to Kimberly to take care of the place when he was out of town, he'd be lucky if Roger's minion wasn't already in his study sorting through his notes.

Finding his own parking space in the underground garage, Jack closed the Jag's door and strode in the direction of the elevator. Damn Roger. Bad enough he'd insisted Jack handle Grant's case, now dear old Dad expected him to baby-sit his protégé.

He'd been putting Kyle off all week. He'd find a way to put him off a little longer. He had important business to handle. A lot more important than listening to Kyle's theories of criminal defense.

So far he'd struck out in his search to find the black car that tried to run Britt down. But he wasn't ready to give up yet. The moment he reached his study, he'd call Nick Clearwater, the private investigator he used to research the few cases he worked in Wisconsin. Nick should be able to provide him with the name of every person who rented a black sedan in the area today. Once he learned who'd tried to run Britt down, he'd notify the police.

Not wanting to wait for the elevator, he used the back stairs. Taking the steps two at a time, he reached the lobby in no time. The sooner he got rid of Kyle, the sooner he could call Clearwater. And the sooner he ensured Britt's safety, the sooner he could ease his mind.

Jack threw open the lobby door and strode in. Sure enough, Kyle sat on the sofa, legs crossed at the ankles, a laptop computer open in his lap. Ever the eager student. This guy showed more ambition than most of Jack's *real* students.

Kyle snapped the folder shut and scrambled to his feet. "Jackson. I need to talk to you. I need you to explain your strategy to me."

Just what he feared. Criminal defense 101. "Some other time, Kyle. I have an urgent matter to take care of." He turned to the elevator and punched the up button. Hopefully Kyle would interpret the action as a dismissal.

Kyle fumbled with the computer. "This is urgent, Jack. I just found out you allowed Grant to meet with the district attorney and I must admit, I'm in the dark as to why."

And he preferred Kyle stay in the dark. "I said, I don't have time."

Kyle marched to the elevator and slapped the file against his open hand. "You'd better make time, damn it."

Jack almost chuckled, but thought better of it. He'd never witnessed so much life in his future brother-in-law. Poor sap. Roger must be riding him awfully hard to inspire that kind of passion.

And then there was Kimberly. She lived and breathed for Kyle, but that didn't mean she wasn't also good at applying a little pressure. As important as this wedding was to her, Kyle was probably turning himself inside out to make her happy.

The elevator slid open and Jack stepped inside. Maybe he should give his future brother-in-law a break. "I have one phone call to make. If you'll take a seat in my living room, I'll take care of my business, then we'll talk."

They rode up to the fifth floor penthouse in silence. Once in his condo, Jack tossed his suit jacket on a chair and marched straight to his study. To his dismay, Kyle followed.

Jack sat behind his desk and picked up his cordless phone. "Kyle, take a seat in the living room."

Kyle shook his head and walked to the window Jack had left open a crack. A stream of sunlight broke through the clouds, glaring off the lenses of his glasses. Jack couldn't see his eyes. But his stiff back and clenched jaw were easy to read. Kyle was upset.

Well, let him be upset in the living room. "My business will take one minute, Kyle. If you want, you can stand right outside the door to make sure I don't sneak out before we have a chance to talk."

Scrutinizing something in the alley below, Kyle didn't answer. Silence blanketed the room, broken only by the hum of traffic, the roll of the whitecaps on the lake, and the clang of a steel garbage Dumpster.

Jack blew a stream of air through tight lips. Kyle was the last person he wanted to deal with right now.

He had tried nice. Now it was time for rude. If he had to remove the pretty-boy lawyer physically, he would do it and ask for Kimberly's forgiveness later. He pushed back his chair and stood. "Kyle, get the hell out of my study."

Kyle nodded his head toward the window. "Does your business involve Tia?"

"Tia? Where in the hell did you get that idea?"

"She's on her way up here."

Jack stood corrected. Kyle wasn't the last person he wanted to deal with, *Tia* was. He set the phone on his desk and raked a hand through his hair.

Kyle spun away from the window. "Maybe she found out you let Grant meet with the D.A. Maybe she thinks you're slitting her husband's throat."

Anger flared in Jack's gut. So much for pitying Kyle. He'd enjoy pounding the tar out of that pretty face, breaking those oh-so-stylish glasses. He balled his hands into fists but then shoved them into his pockets.

He wasn't angry with Kyle. Roger was the one he should pound the tar out of for saddling him with his flunky. Jack already spent two days a week teaching law. He didn't have the patience for another pupil.

Or the time. He glanced at his watch. Four-thirty. Clearwater's office closed at five for the weekend. If he didn't call before then, he'd have to track the poor guy down at home.

The shrill screech of the buzzer shredded the quiet. Jack flinched inwardly at the sound. The buzzer sounded again. Knowing Tia, she'd lean on the button until Jack buzzed her in.

He groaned. The more the merrier. He pulled himself out of his chair and strode to the security panel near the door. Glancing at Tia's angry face in the video monitor, he hit the button, buzzing her in.

It didn't take long for Tia to storm through his study door, face red as her flashing fingernails. "Jackson, you rat. What do you think you're trying to do?" The smell of French Bordeaux tainted the air in her wake.

Jack sighed and walked back to his desk. He'd give Tia and Kyle five minutes to vent their grievances. After that, he'd remove them bodily if he had to. "All right, Tia. Don't be shy. Out with it."

Tia frowned at his sarcasm and stomped her foot like the spoiled child she was. "You know damn well what's going on. You forced Grant to talk with that witch. She wants to put him in jail, and you're trying to help her."

Jack rolled his eyes. Tia was being her usual hysterical self, flying off the handle before she knew what she was talking about. "Grant talked to Assistant D.A. Gerritsen in order to buy some time."

Kyle stepped closer to Tia and placed a quieting hand on her shoulder. He frowned at Jack. "What do you mean, buy time?"

Might as well level with them. "Exactly that. I made a deal with Britt. I allowed her to talk to Grant, and she agreed to leave Grant and the family alone."

Kyle nodded as if fascinated with the strategy. "For how long?"

"Until after your wedding. That should give us enough time to put a serious dent in what little evidence she has. If we can do that, we can prevent her from filing charges. I don't have to explain what that means to Grant's career."

A light of understanding flashed in Kyle's eyes. "So that's why Grant agreed to go along with it."

Jack nodded. A star student. Maybe Kyle wasn't as vacant as he'd originally believed.

Tia shook her head, her bobbed black hair tousling into her eyes. She pushed it back with her scarlet-tipped fingers. "I don't trust her. What's keeping her from reneging on the deal?"

Funny, Jack had never considered the possibility of Britt not honoring their deal. It was a waste of time to consider it now. "I know her. She'll keep her word."

Tia threw her head back and laughed, bitter as bile. "You know her, all right. All you men are the same. You were born with a perfectly good head on your shoulders. Try using *it* to think for a change."

Jack sat down in his chair and said nothing. He'd learned long ago there was no point in arguing with his sister-in-law. She had a right to be bitter. Not even all that Alcott money could make up for the embarrassment and pain of a philandering husband.

Tia stormed toward him. Apparently, she wasn't finished. "What if Britt uses that time to find more evidence against Grant? What if your little plan backfires?"

"If more evidence exists, Britt will find it whether she charges Grant first, or not." Jack studied Tia. It was unlikely a prolonged investigation would turn up more evidence against an innocent man. And Grant had a lot of faults, but he was no murderer. Jack was sure of it. "Are you saying you think Grant is guilty, Tia?"

Her dark eyes widened and she stepped backward, bumping into Kyle. "I didn't—of course not."

A cold lump settled in Jack's stomach. He'd spent hours grilling Tia and Grant after the blackmail surprise, and they still hadn't told him the whole truth. Worse than that, he had the uneasy feeling they'd out-and-out lied to him. And to the authorities. "You told the police you were with Grant at the time of the murder. That's a lie, isn't it? You didn't see him after you left the convention center, did you?"

Fear glistened in her eyes. She twirled her wedding ring with a fingernail. She looked to Kyle, as if imploring him to bail her out of this latest lie.

Kyle held his hands up, palms toward her. "We're Grant's lawyers, Tia. You have to level with us so we can help him."

She focused once again on Jack. Her shoulders slumped in resignation. "I didn't see him. I was upset. I went for a drive."

Jack held up a finger. He wanted to get this new story crystal clear in his mind. "You never went home after you stormed out of the convention center?"

"I went for a drive."

"What time did you get home?"

"I didn't go home. I was upset."

Strain besieged the back of Jack's neck. If this story grew any worse, he'd have one hell of a tension headache. "So you didn't see him all night?"

"No. I stayed in a hotel."

Jack couldn't believe his ears. "You stayed in a hotel? What were you thinking?"

Tia threw up her arms and stomped across the study. "I was angry. Wouldn't you be? He just told me he was having an affair. That slut was carrying his child. His *baby*." Stopping dead, she clutched her abdomen with both hands and tears poured from her eyes.

Kyle slipped a comforting arm around her shoulder and escorted her to the couch.

"I didn't know he'd kill her. How could I know? I thought he was going to leave me for her." She gasped for breath, choking on her tears.

Jack just stared. "Why didn't you tell me this? Why in hell did you lie to the police? Didn't it occur to you they would find out? One call to your credit card company, and Grant's alibi is out the window. Unless, you paid with cash?"

She shook her head, her tears coming in waves of sobs.

Of course she wouldn't use cash. Tia loved her plastic. He felt like punching something. "I don't believe this."

Kyle patted Tia's shoulder as if he didn't quite know what to do. "Don't worry, Tia. Jack isn't trying to attack you. We're on your side. We'll figure out something."

Jack leaned forward. Elbows on desk, he supported his aching head with his hands. Hell, he understood Tia's anguish. She and Grant had been trying to have a baby for years. She was used to his tawdry affairs, but Tangi's pregnancy had obviously crushed her.

Suspicion crowded into his mind. Maybe Tia had a role in Tangi's death. Sure she said she believed Grant did it, but Tia had lied to him all along. Why would she start telling the truth now? She certainly had a motive. And since she and Grant weren't together that night, she had the opportunity as well.

Listening to Tia's quiet sobs and Kyle's calming tone, Jack shook his head. He didn't want to give voice to his suspicions. He just couldn't accept the whole idea that a member of the family could be a murderer.

His head throbbed as if pinched in a vise. Sure Tia was a different animal from Grant. Unlike his weak passivity, she had plenty of guts and passion. Her drinking only made her more volatile, more gutsy. If backed into a corner, maybe Tia could kill. But that didn't mean she had. He thought of the questions Britt had fired at Grant moments before he rushed out of the restaurant. Britt couldn't be right about Tia, could she?

Britt.

He still hadn't called the private investigator. The driver of the black sedan could be plotting his next attack this very minute. An invisible hand gripped Jack's heart and squeezed. Five years ago, he'd given Britt up to protect her. He couldn't live with himself if he allowed some punk to hurt her now.

The phone on his desk rang before he could pick up the receiver. He answered it. "Jackson Alcott."

"Jack?" a faint voice squeaked through static.

"Kimberly?"

Kyle stood and stepped toward the desk, his hand out for the phone.

Jack ignored him. "Kimberly? I can hardly hear you. Where are you?"

"Thank God you're home, Jack." Her voice sounded desperate and tinny, as if she were calling him from the depths of an abandoned well. Or from her car phone.

"Are you looking for Kyle?"

"No, I want to talk to you."

Jack shook his head at Kyle.

Kyle's handsome face sagged with disappointment. He returned to the couch, sitting next to a sniffling Tia.

"I'm on my car phone. You'll never guess who I passed on Farwell Drive."

Jack searched his mind and came up with nothing. He didn't have any idea what she was referring to nor why her call was so urgent. "Who?"

"Britt. She's on her way to the house."

The news hit Jack with all the force of a kick in the gut. Something stirred inside him. Something close to fear. "Who's home right now?"

"Mom is at the Country Club and Tia and Grant are both out. The only one home is Daddy."

Roger. Exactly what he feared. He couldn't let Britt talk to Roger. There was no telling what secrets Roger would let slip just for his own cruel amusement. He had to stop her. "Thanks for calling, Kimberly. I'll try to head her off."

"You won't be able to, Jack. She's ringing the doorbell as we speak. Do you want me to see if I can stall her until you get here?"

He'd just made a deal with Britt to keep Kimberly out of this mess. He couldn't involve his sister now. "No, Kimberly. I'll take care of it."

He hung up the phone and bolted for the door, ignoring Tia and Kyle's exclamations. His phone call to Clearwater would have to wait. Damn. He had no time to lose, no time to usher out Tia and Kyle, and no way of knowing what Roger would say to Britt.

He had to stop her from talking to Roger before it was too late.

BRITT SWUNG her car into the Alcotts' cobblestone drive. The sun sank low in the west and sparkled off

Lake Mendota's waves, cloaking the front of the house in shadow. One glimpse of the impenetrable brick facade and imposing pillars, and a chill crept up her back. She tried to shake it off, but the chill lingered, working deep into her bones until every joint ached.

She must be crazy coming here, facing Roger Alcott alone, no matter how much she needed answers. She'd wanted to bring Mylinski with her, but when she'd called Roger to set up a meeting, he'd insisted she come solo. She'd been foolish to agree.

At least Jack wasn't here. She'd scanned the driveway before she'd driven in. No green Jaguar. She could take comfort in that. And she needed comfort right now, from whatever source she could find.

With the mention of one name, Marcus Spinnetti had destroyed her hopes of putting the past, and Jack, safely behind her. Roger had paid Tangi's debt. The Alcott family was involved in Tangi's death, all right. Deeply involved.

She climbed out of her car. Straightening her trench coat, she approached the formidable front door. She'd give almost anything to just turn around and walk away. To never confront another Alcott.

Maybe she should take her dad's advice and turn the case over to someone else. Dillon Reese handled most of the homicide cases in the D.A.'s office. Shrewd, tireless, and focused like a laser, the transplanted Texan was the most driven person she'd ever met. He would do a good job on Tangi's case. A great job, in fact. She could climb back into her car, drive back to the office, and turn the file over to him. She'd never have to deal with Jack or his family again.

She swallowed around the lump in her throat. She couldn't do that. She'd made a promise to Tangi. And no matter what, she'd fulfill that promise. She couldn't live with herself if she didn't.

She stepped onto the massive front porch and approached the ornate door. The doorbell button glowed with a clear white light in the dark shadow of the house. She reached toward the button and paused to take a deep breath. Yes, she had to talk to Roger Alcott. She had to find out why he'd paid Tangi's debt. She pushed the button.

A bell pealed through the house, a slow heavy chime like a death knell. Sheer force of will kept her standing on the porch, waiting.

The door swung open and Roger himself stood before her.

Her mouth went dry.

He said nothing, just looked her up and down with those cold, almost-black eyes. He seemed to take in everything about her, from her shoe size to who she'd voted for in the last election.

She stood straight and tall, as if she welcomed his scrutiny. She didn't dare hide from this man, didn't dare flinch. Like a hungry wolf, he would attack at the smallest sign of weakness or fear.

And Roger Alcott always went for the jugular.

Finally, he stepped aside and motioned her into the entrance hall. "Come in, Britt. It has been a long time."

She stepped inside, her heels clicking on the gray marble floor. The sound echoed through the cavernlike hall. The heavy brass chandelier loomed overhead like a suspended guillotine. The grand white staircase wrapped around the hall like a cobra ready to strike. It had been a long time since she'd set foot in this house all right, and she'd missed its interior about as much as she'd missed its inhabitants. "I have some questions I'd like to ask you."

Roger smiled, showing his straight white teeth, and she couldn't help thinking of Red Riding Hood's Big Bad Wolf. "So you want to get down to business right away. I always liked that about you, Britt. May I call you Britt, or do we have to be formal since you're here in an official capacity?"

She bristled at his mocking tone. "You can call me anything you like as long as you answer my questions."

"And if I don't?"

"Then I'm afraid you'll have to go downtown with me and answer Detective Mylinski's questions. And take my word for it, your home is much more comfortable than a police interrogation room."

His smile widened. "Downtown, huh?"

"Yes."

"We'll see. For now, will my study do?" He turned and motioned for her to join him.

She followed him through the endless halls. They passed the dining room where she'd suffered through many Alcott family dinners, the parlor overlooking Lake Mendota's crashing waves, and the powder room where she'd gotten sick the first time she met Jack's father.

She could still hear echoes of his grilling questions, his scalding insults. She'd been just out of law school and naive as Red Riding Hood herself. Since then, she'd learned to deal with people like Roger. She'd learned to hold her own.

Finally, they entered Roger's study.

She'd never been in this room before. Uneasiness hovered over her like the fog of cigar smoke in the air. The room was just how she'd imagined. Like Roger, every stick of furniture and scrap of rug emitted the oppressive aura of power.

"Please take off your coat. Apparently, we have a lot to talk about."

She did as he invited, draping her coat on the arm of a leather wing chair. A hungry inferno blazed in the oversized black marble fireplace, sending tongues of heat to every corner of the room. Despite the fire, a shiver spread over her skin. No amount of warmth could dispel the chill of Roger Alcott's presence.

He motioned to a couch, and she sat, its slick leather swallowing her up.

"Would you like a drink, Britt?"

"No, thank you."

He opened a small refrigerator that blended in with the knotty pine paneling. "If I remember, you usually drank club soda." He pronounced the words with disdain, as if anyone not strong enough to drink straight whiskey didn't deserve to live.

She flashed him a phony smile. "You have a good memory, Roger. But if you don't mind, I'd prefer to skip the pleasantries and get to the reason I'm here."

He held up a finger, frowning down at her as if he were reprimanding a stupid child. "First things first."

He took out a bottle of club soda and twisted off the cap, the carbonation hissing free. He filled a glass with ice from a brass bucket and set the bottle and glass on the marble-topped table in front of her. After pouring himself three fingers of whiskey, he settled into one of the leather wing chairs. His back to the fire, he sipped his drink, his eyes cloaked in shadow. "Now, why are you here, Britt?"

She drew herself up and set her chin. "We have a man in custody, a Marcus Spinnetti, who claims you paid him a great deal of money."

Roger raised an eyebrow. "And what is a great deal of money to you, Britt?"

"Twenty thousand dollars."

"Hmm. No wonder Jackson dated you. You're easy to impress."

Anger bubbled deep inside her. The bitter flavor of hatred filled her mouth. She wanted to tell him exactly what she thought of him. Instead, she sipped her club soda and crossed her legs. She had to keep her emotions under control. She was here to get answers, not revenge. "Why did you pay him the money?"

"I never said I did." He opened a carved wood box on the marble table and pulled out a cigar. He carried out the ritual of lighting it and puffed a stifling cloud of smoke into the air. "Does Neil Fitzroy know you're here?"

Britt couldn't keep herself from inwardly cringing. Of course District Attorney Fitzroy didn't know she was here. He was so immersed in his upcoming campaign, he probably didn't realize she was working this case. No doubt he'd be livid if he knew.

"He doesn't know, does he? No. Fitz would never go along with something like this. Maybe I'll give him a call." Rising from his chair, Roger reached for the sleek black phone sitting on the ebony bar.

She couldn't let him call the D.A. At the very least, Fitzroy would yank her off Tangi's case. At most, she'd be searching for another job. She lifted her chin.

Stay calm, stay cool. "I don't think it would be in your son's best interest to do that."

He paused midreach, his thin lips twisting into a vicious smile. "Really?"

"Jack and I have a deal. He allowed me to interview Grant this noon. In return, I've agreed to lay off Grant until after Kim's wedding. I don't have to explain what that means to Grant's case, do I? If I find proof he's innocent or evidence implicating another suspect during that time, Grant will be home free. I doubt some other attorney would agree to honor that deal."

Roger raised his glass to his lips and sipped, his expression unreadable.

She couldn't tell if her strategy had worked or not. There was one way to find out. "Why did you pay Marcus Spinnetti the twenty thousand dollars?"

He sat back in his chair, puffing his cigar and drinking his whiskey. "I always liked you."

Britt braced herself. He was playing with her the way a cat plays with a mouse before he pounces. She had no idea where Roger was leading, but she had a definite feeling she wouldn't like it. Not one bit.

"You're good-looking, intelligent, ambitious. But I couldn't let Jack marry you. Nothing against my son's authority, but you're just too unmanageable." He waved his cigar, a trail of smoke hanging in the air behind it. "Besides, he's an Alcott. He can do a lot better than the daughter of a crippled cop."

Loathing churned in Britt's stomach. She didn't need him to remind her of Jack's betrayal, and she didn't need his insults. That crippled cop was worth fifty Roger Alcotts. She clutched her glass so hard, the cut crystal dug into her palms. Catching herself, she forced a bored sigh. "Really, Roger. I'd hoped we could avoid the name-calling this time. Is there a point to this?"

He blew a puff of putrid smoke into the air. "When your fixation on Grant began, I decided to hold off on calling Fitz. At the very least, I hoped Jack could control you. Apparently this little bargain the two of you cooked up was his attempt. But I'm afraid I can't leave things to chance any longer. I have no choice but to make that phone call."

She set her drink on the table and pressed her palms against her thighs to keep her hands from shaking. Angry tears surged at the back of her eyes. She pushed them back and raised her chin.

Roger would carry out his threat if she didn't halt her investigation of Grant. Of this, she had no doubt. If he called D.A. Fitzroy, she'd lose control of Tangi's case. She'd probably lose the career she'd worked so hard to build.

All she had to do to avoid this fate was to stop investigating Grant. If she did this one thing, she'd never have to deal with Jack or his family again. She'd save her career. She'd save her heart.

But she'd lose her soul.

"Go ahead and call. The case will be reassigned to Dillon Reese. He's not any easier to deal with than I am."

Roger's scowl filled her with satisfaction. Apparently, he hadn't expected her to stand up to him. He stood and paced the length of the room, puffing on his cigar. He stopped his pacing in front of the fire, turned to her, and smiled. "What reason did Jack give you for breaking your engagement?"

Startled, Britt couldn't find her voice. What was

Roger getting at? He more than anyone should know why Jack broke their engagement. He had been the one pulling Jack's strings the night of the engagement party. And every night since.

A sharp pain twisted in her chest. She steeled herself against its familiar throb. Jack's reasons didn't matter to her anymore. He'd betrayed her, pure and simple. And she would never let him do it again. She set her chin. "He did it so he could take his proper place in the family—defending your business associates in court, dating their daughters—under your thumb. Just where you wanted him, Roger."

She leaned back in the couch and tried to read Roger's shadowed eyes. After five years, nothing he could tell her about Jack could hurt her. So why was he staring at her like a wolf eyeing his prey? And why did her stomach seize with queasy fear?

"And you believed his loyal son act? Didn't his change of heart toward me seem a bit sudden?"

She fought the urge to worry her bottom lip. At first Jack's pronouncement had seemed totally baffling and out of character to her. He'd never gone along with his father's twisted judgement on anything. Certainly not something as important as their life together. She hadn't believed it. But that was before she'd heard he'd taken on the airtight racketeering case against one of Roger's more notorious Chicago business associates, Rico Gianni. And before she'd seen Jack smiling at her from the front page of the *State Journal,* shmoozing at the annual Frosty Ball, Gianni's daughter on his arm.

The wolf smiled, showing his teeth. "I can see those gears turning in your head. You'd like to know the real reason for Jack's change of heart, wouldn't you?''

She shook her head. It had happened five years ago. She was over Jack. Over the pain. Over the anguish. She didn't want to revisit his betrayal. Especially not with Roger. ''I'd like to stick to the original subject. What does this have to do with my investigation?''

''Once you hear Jack's real reason, the rest will be very clear to you. You see, Jack was hiding something from you. He didn't want you to learn the truth.''

Her mind whirled with questions. She wanted to grab Roger by the throat and shake him until he stopped playing games. Until he told her everything. She struggled to hold on to her composure. ''What truth?''

''Have you ever wondered how a cop could save enough money to send his daughter to law school?''

The throb of her pulse rose in her ears. ''What are you talking about?''

The door burst open. Jack strode into the room and straight toward her. ''Not another word, Roger.''

Britt bit her lip. Roger was about to lay his cards on the table. How dare Jack barge in? ''Jack. What are you doing here?''

Jack grabbed her upper arms, his fingers digging into her flesh. ''It's time for you to leave.''

She braced herself, trying to wrest her arms from his grasp.

He was too strong. He dragged her out of the soft couch. Setting her on her feet, he propelled her toward the door.

Past Roger puffing on his cigar, a smile twisting his lips.

Chapter Eight

Mind reeling, Britt fought to wrench her arm from Jack's bruising grip. "What the hell do you think you're doing? Let me go."

He didn't answer. Holding her fast, he propelled her through the kitchen and out the nearest door. He forced her to the far edge of the patio, turned her to face him, and pinned her between the railing and his body.

He loomed over her, his dark glare cutting, his face hard. His body heat burned into her, firing the heat of her anger like a match to gasoline.

"Your coat. Where's your coat?"

The wrought iron dug into her back. The October wind blasted off the lake, ripping her hair loose from its ribbon and sending strands slashing across her cheeks. "Where do you think my coat is? You didn't give me a chance to gather my things."

Jack spun away from her and strode back to the house. The door slammed behind him.

She clenched her teeth until they ached. What had Roger been about to say? What was Jack so afraid she'd hear?

She wanted to march right back in that house and

rant and rave and demand the truth. But that would just give Jack an excuse to manhandle her again. And Roger more reason to sneer.

She turned away from the house and leaned against the railing. The orange sunset bounced off the crashing whitecaps, turning the waves into tongues of flame. The sunset's fire paled in comparison to the fury smoldering inside her.

Roger had been so close to telling her the real reason Jack had broken their engagement five years ago. So close.

A small part of her cringed. Maybe she didn't want to know. Maybe she was better off in the dark, believing the bogus story Jack had given her.

No.

Her anger swelled, blocking the pain, the uncertainty. *No one* was better off in the dark. Hadn't she learned that when her mother died? Hadn't she seen it again when Tangi died? Both deaths had cheated her, left her in the dark, searching for answers.

She had the right to know the real reason he'd broken their engagement. Only by knowing the truth could she make her own decisions. And she had the right to make her own decisions. No matter what.

The door slammed again. Jack.

Clenching her teeth, she continued to stare out at the waves.

He loomed behind her, his power, his anger, his heat. He draped her trench coat over her shoulders. "Damn it, Britt. Why did you come here? Why did you have to talk to Roger?"

She turned to face him, meeting his dark eyes. All the pain of the last five years settled in her chest. Heavy. Bitter. She struggled to breathe. "Tell me the truth, Jack. Why did you break off our engagement? Why did you let me believe you were under your father's thumb? Why did you defend that crook and date his daughter? Why did you do those things?''

Jack looked away from her, his eyes scanning the waves. He stood silent. For how long, Britt could only guess. The sun slipped closer to the horizon. Lights blinked from the Capitol dome and along the lakeshore of the Madison isthmus.

Ice crept into her bones. Cold and alone, she slipped her arms into the sleeves of her coat, wrapping its warmth around her. She set her chin. ''The silent treatment won't work. I want the truth. You owe me that much.''

''You should never have come here. Roger should never—''

''Jack, I deserve to know. Roger said you were keeping something from me. A secret.''

Glancing over his shoulder at the house, he claimed her arm, his grip gentle but uncompromising. ''Let's take a walk.''

Apparently, he wanted her out of Roger's range. A point she wouldn't argue. She walked alongside him to the water's edge, autumn leaves crackling underfoot. Her trench coat flapped in the gusts like a weather-beaten flag.

Reaching the fire pit, he ushered her behind its fieldstone chimney and out of the wind's path.

She leaned back against the rough-hewn stone and tried to read the expression on his face. Sadness creased his forehead. Conflict gleamed in his eyes. Whatever the real reason he'd broken up with her, whatever his secret, it tore him apart.

''Tell me.''

He shook his head. Twilight glinted off his dark hair.

Foreboding inched up her spine. She shoved it away. She had to know the truth. No matter how well-intentioned, secrets were like malignancies, growing and spreading until they blotted out everything good. "What are you afraid of? Are you worried that if I know the truth, you won't be able to control me?"

"Control you? I've never wanted to control you." Jack's frown deepened to a glower. "I suppose Roger told you that, too."

"Among other things."

"And you believe him?"

Roger? Not if he insisted the earth was round. But where did that leave her? Could she trust Jack?

She peered into Jack's eyes, so deep and dark. A sliver of heat shot through her. She knew him. Five years was a long time, but she still *knew* him. She knew what made him angry. She knew what made him laugh. And if the Jack Alcott she knew kept a secret, he kept it to protect someone. In this case, that someone had to be her. "You broke off our engagement to protect me, didn't you? What did you think you were protecting me *from?*"

A muscle twitched in his jaw. His dark eyes flashed with anger. "Damn Roger. I gave up everything so you wouldn't find out. Everything."

"Jack, tell me." Her voice barely rose above a husky whisper. She had to know. Whatever the consequences, she had to know.

He said nothing. He just stood there, staring at her, his jaw tight, his forehead creased in anguish.

The overpowering heat of him, the leather-and-musk scent of him, made her head whirl. Memories jumbled her mind. Slow walks through the pine forest. The smoldering passion in his eyes. The way he held her hand as if it was the most precious thing in the world.

She closed her mind. She couldn't bear the pain. If she remembered how it felt to *have* these things, she'd have to remember how it felt to *lose* them. "Jack, I..."

Moving his hand to her face, he traced the line of her cheekbone with his fingertips. "I never wanted to hurt you, Britt. It killed me to walk away." He leaned close. Close enough for her to feel his warm breath on her face. Close enough to kiss her.

Automatically she tilted her head back and parted her lips. She wanted his kiss. God help her, she wanted it.

But she couldn't let him kiss her. She needed the truth. She pressed her back against the cold stone. "Why, Jack? Why did you walk away?"

"I couldn't live with the alternative."

"What alternative?"

He stepped back. Shadow shrouded his eyes. His hands balled into fists at his sides. "Damn Roger." His voice was dead. Cold. "Damn him to hell."

Light glittered from the windows of the Alcott house. Although the house rose two hundred feet away, she and Jack seemed isolated, alone. "*Tell* me."

The muscle twitched along his jaw. "I lied when I told you that business about taking my place in the family. And for the record, I never defended Gianni. I just told a few select people I was his counsel so the news would get back to you. And I took his daughter to the Frosty Ball so you would believe it was over between us.''

"Why?"

"Because Roger threatened to use his contacts to ensure you would never get a job as a prosecutor. And he could do it, Britt. I knew how hard you worked, how talented you were. I couldn't let him do that to you.''

Her job. Roger had threatened her job. Her stomach clenched with hatred. No wonder Jack had felt he had to do something to protect her. He'd always understood how important her job was to her. The only things more important were her family and, at that time, Jack. But her job alone wouldn't have been enough to make him walk away. He still wasn't telling her everything. "And the secret? What is the secret Roger referred to?''

Even though shadow hid his eyes, she could sense him look away.

Frustration hummed in her ears. Didn't he see what he was doing? "You can't protect me from the truth, Jack. All you're doing is preventing me from drawing my own conclusions, making my own decisions.''

His eyebrows rose. "I don't see it that way."

Of course he didn't. He couldn't see it any way but his own. Tears turned the world into a blurred mosaic of light and blackness. She struggled to blink back the deluge. The last thing she wanted was to expose her weakness to him.

Why couldn't he understand where she was coming from? With Roger for a father, Jack had suffered a thousand kinds of betrayal. He'd spent most of his life protecting his mother, his sister, and even Grant from Roger's manipulations. Why couldn't he see that withholding the truth was as bad as a lie?

Britt dug her fingernails into the scrapes on her hands, pain cutting through the frustration jumbling her mind. Of course he couldn't understand. He hadn't been there when her mother broke the news from her hospital bed. He hadn't seen her waste away and die in a matter of weeks. "You can't protect me with secrets, Jack. All you do is hurt me."

He shook his head and let out an exasperated sigh. "I'm keeping you from being hurt."

"That's what my mother thought. She knew she had cancer months before she died, but she didn't tell us." Britt stopped, surprised by the venom in her voice.

She swallowed the bitter lump in her throat and plunged ahead. "Mom wanted to protect Dad and me. She thought she could shield us from the pain." She laughed, the sound brittle in the cold night air.

He grasped her hand in his.

Warmth crept up her arm at his touch. She dragged in a deep breath. She didn't want his sympathy. She wanted him to understand. "My mother didn't protect us from anything. She cheated us of the time we had left with her."

"She cared about you. She didn't want to—"

She ripped her hand from his grasp. He didn't understand a thing she was saying. "She didn't want to monopolize my time. She didn't want to burden me. *Those* were her reasons."

Jack frowned. He *still* didn't understand.

"Don't you see? My mother should have respected me enough to know I could handle the truth."

She had to get away from him. She couldn't bear

to explain any more. Couldn't bear the misdirected sympathy in his eyes. She slipped out between Jack and the fire pit's chimney and strode toward the crashing waves. The wind battered her, lashing the escaped strands of her hair against her cheeks like dozens of tiny whips. Its savagery felt good, felt right.

Jack fell in close beside her, his voice rising into the wind. "Right or wrong, your mother tried to spare you."

She whirled to face him, her heart's thud eclipsing the roar of the waves. The anger she'd harbored since her mother's death tore loose from its moorings. "I could have spent more time with my mother. I could have helped her. She had no right to take that away from me. She had no right to deprive me of the truth. And neither do you."

He clenched his jaw, his face haunted, tired. "It's not my secret to tell."

Rage screeched in Britt's ears. Hadn't he heard one word? How could he do this? She raised her fists and slammed them against his hard chest. She wanted to hurt him like he'd hurt her. Like her mother had hurt her. Like Tangi had hurt her.

He grabbed her wrists, his grip as tight as handcuffs.

Her hands stung. Tears streamed down her cheeks in hot rivers. She had to know. "Tell me, Jack. Tell me the truth."

He released her wrists, his dark eyes peering into her soul. "I'm sorry, Britt. It's not my secret to tell. If you want the truth, you'll have to ask your father."

"My father? What does my father have to do with this?"

"It's your father's secret, Britt. And he'll have to tell you."

Roger's words echoed through her mind. *Have you ever wondered how a cop could save enough money to send his daughter to law school?*

For a moment, her heart seemed to stop beating.

"Go ask your father, Britt."

She looked into Jack's eyes. His worry, his fear for her scared her to death. Insides trembling, she drew herself up. She glanced over her shoulder at the Alcott mansion. Roger's connection to Spinnetti would have to wait. Now she needed to ask her father for the truth. The truth couldn't be worse than not knowing.

Could it?

BRITT PULLED INTO her driveway and stopped in front of the garage, turning off the ignition. Light glowed from the living room windows, the multicolored flicker of the television screen bouncing off the Japanese yew outside. Dad was home early from his big euchre tournament at the VFW. Good.

A shiver of cowardice worked its way from her heart to the tips of her toes. Even Jack was afraid. Afraid of her learning the truth. Afraid of hurting her further.

Before he'd let her go, he had insisted he follow her home. She'd refused his offer. She wanted to be alone to confront her dad. She didn't need Jack to witness her pain.

She shoved open the car door and climbed out into the night. The oak overhead swayed in the wind, its few remaining leaves succumbing to the cold blast one by one. Swallowing her dread, she headed up the walk and unlocked the front door. She paused before slipping inside. She couldn't let fear get in the way. She'd talk to her father, force him to tell her his secret.

She opened the door and stepped inside, her heels clicking on the hardwood floor and echoing through the tiny foyer. Television voices drifted from the living room. She headed in that direction.

Dad slumped in his wheelchair in front of the tube, his head drooped forward, his chin touching his chest. His shallow snore rose above the television sound.

Odd. She glanced at her watch. He couldn't have been home from the tournament very long. And he never fell asleep in front of the television. In fact, he'd suffered from insomnia since the shooting that claimed the use of his legs. He rarely slept at all.

She circled the couch and bent over his slumbering form. She'd have to wake him. She couldn't live with this secret hanging over her head one minute longer.

"Dad?"

He didn't move.

"Dad? Wake up."

Nothing.

She shook his arm.

His head lolled to the side, but he didn't stir.

Fear jolted her like an electrical charge. Was something wrong with him? He couldn't be drunk, could he? He never drank while playing cards. He said it interfered with his stratagem. Except for a few beers during Green Bay Packer football games, he didn't drink at all. She leaned close to him and smelled his breath. No scent of alcohol.

Standing over him, she grabbed both of his arms and shook. "Wake up, Dad. Wake up."

His eyelids fluttered open, but his blue eyes didn't seem to focus on her face.

"Dad? What's wrong?"

He mumbled something unintelligible, then stared at her like she was a stranger.

Dread rose in her like flood waters. "Dad? It's Britt. Can you hear me?"

Understanding dawned in his eyes. He nodded. "Britt, hon."

"Are you sick? How do you feel?" She pressed her hand to his forehead. Maybe a little warm, but not a full-blown fever. Could he be having a heart attack? A stroke?

"Is your mother home yet?"

Alarm gripped Britt's heart like an icy hand. "What are you talking about? Mom died three years ago."

His eyebrows pulled together in a frown. "I'm tired. Tired. Tell your mother I just want to sleep." His eyes closed and his head slumped forward.

Panic scrambled up her spine. Something was wrong. She had to get help.

She raced out of the living room to the kitchen and grabbed the cordless phone off the countertop. Punching in the numbers, she returned to the living room, praying for the dispatcher to hurry.

"Nine-one-one."

"I just got home and found my father ill. I need an ambulance." She gave her address and explained his symptoms.

"What kind of heating system do you have in the house, ma'am?"

Britt shook her head. Maybe she hadn't heard the woman right. "Heating system? Why?"

"Do you have forced air heat?"

She thought of the furnace in the basement. "Yes. Forced air."

"Are you suffering from a headache, ma'am?"

"No."

"Are you nauseated at all?"

Britt circled her arm around her middle. Her stomach was queasy. She'd assumed the nausea was a result of her panic. "A little, yes."

"Can you remove yourself and your father from the premises?"

She eyed her dad, slumping in the wheelchair. "Yes. My father is in a wheelchair."

"Then do so immediately. Go to a neighbor's house and wait for the ambulance. It'll be there in a few minutes. Make sure both you and your father are warm and get plenty of fresh air. You may be suffering from carbon monoxide poisoning."

Carbon monoxide poisoning? Britt murmured something into the phone, turned it off, and stuffed it into the pocket of her coat. She needed to clear her mind. She needed to think. She needed to get out, ASAP.

She dashed to her bedroom and ripped the down comforter from her bed. Returning to the living room, she draped it over her dad. That should keep him warm. Now for the fresh air.

Her pulse pounded in her ears. A shadow of pain throbbed behind her eyes with each squeeze of her heart. Clutching the handles of the wheelchair, she pushed her father into the foyer, threw the front door open, and wheeled him out onto the porch.

She scooped fresh, frigid air into her lungs. The wind whipped the comforter, sending the corners flapping. She tucked the edges around him. She closed the door to the house, locking the poisonous air inside.

She clawed open the collar of his shirt. Where was that damned ambulance?

A green Jaguar sat under a streetlight in front of her house. Jack.

He dashed across the lawn toward her. His arms encircled her, guiding her to a sitting position on the front step. "What's happened, Britt? What's wrong?"

Tears welled behind her eyes, but she ordered them back. She gripped the edge of the cement step, steadying herself. "Dad. He passed out. They think it might be carbon monoxide poisoning."

"They?"

"Nine-one-one."

Jack bent over her father, lowering his ear within inches of his mouth.

Somewhere in the distance, a siren screamed, piercing the terror swirling in Britt's head. "He's still breathing, isn't he?"

Jack nodded. "Barely."

A shudder shook her from head to toe. He could die. Her dad could die. She could lose him like she'd lost her mom, like she'd lost Tangi. She gasped for air, but tears choked her, reducing her to a spasm of sputtering hiccups.

He couldn't die. She couldn't lose her father, too. She drew in a breath. Before she could draw another, an ambulance screeched around the turn in the road and roared into her driveway.

Please God, don't let them be too late. She closed her eyes, vaguely aware of the tears flowing down her cheeks.

Chapter Nine

Jack shifted on the rock-hard hospital chair. His legs ached to stand, to move, to *do* something. He'd already taken three trips to the cafeteria only to return empty-handed, his stomach too riled to digest anything resembling food. He'd already bothered the poor nurses so many times their flirtatious glances had long since changed to annoyed glares. And he sure as hell couldn't march into ICU and demand to see Britt and her father again. The last time he'd tried that a nurse had thrown him out on his ear.

Britt would be all right. She hadn't been exposed to the carbon monoxide long. But Lars was another story. From all indications, Britt's father was in serious trouble.

She must be beside herself with worry. He could still picture the way her lips had parted when he stroked her satin cheek, still see the passion shining in her vibrant blue eyes, hot as lasers. She was the same as she'd been five years ago. Explosive. Passionate. All woman.

God, he'd missed her.

Pain stabbed his chest. The secret still hung over his head like a shroud. Lars hadn't been able to tell

Britt. And Jack couldn't tell her. The secret stood between them, keeping them apart as effectively as it had separated them five years ago.

Hell, who was he kidding? Lars's secret wasn't some wall separating impassioned lovers. All their problems wouldn't disappear the moment the secret saw the light of day. In fact, once Britt learned what he'd kept from her, she'd never forgive him. Even though he had done it to protect her and her father.

So why was he sitting on a stone-cold chair in a hospital corridor at midnight?

Because Britt was in danger, that's why. Somebody had tried to kill her. Twice now. And she was too damned headstrong to protect herself.

Jack shifted again on the chair. He'd seen the police detective walk into the ICU, the line of his mouth grim, his eyes all business. With a few well-placed phone calls, Jack had learned the police had been swarming Britt's little house most of the night looking for evidence. And they'd found it. A jimmied lock. Several holes punched into the furnace's heat exchanger. This carbon monoxide poisoning incident was no accident. Britt's furnace hadn't developed a leak of its own volition. Somehow, someone had sneaked into Britt's house and sabotaged it while Britt and Lars were out. And he'd bet his life that same someone had rented a black car this afternoon.

Misgivings skittered through Jack's mind. Could these attempts on Britt's life be tied to Tangi Rowe's murder? And if they were, could a member of his own family be responsible?

The weight of suspicion hit him full in the chest. God knew his family was screwed up. But was one of them a murderer?

Had Roger, Grant, or Tia rented the black car? Had one of them sabotaged Britt's furnace? All three had a big reason for wanting Britt out of the way. Britt's investigation threatened to destroy Grant. But would any of them try to kill Britt? Had one of them killed Tangi?

He buried his head in his hands. He still didn't believe Grant capable of murder. But Roger? Or Tia? God help him, he didn't know. He didn't seem to know anything anymore.

But if he was going to protect Britt, he'd have to find out.

And he would protect Britt. Of this, he had no doubt. He'd protect her whether she wanted him to or not.

BRITT GRIMACED and looked up into the worried blue eyes of Al Mylinski. Her pulse kept time with the whooshing rhythm of her dad's respirator. "What are you trying to say, Al?"

"Someone jimmied the lock on your basement door and rapped holes in your furnace's heat exchanger. Carbon monoxide spilled into the air ducts instead of going up the chimney."

"And it circulated through the house."

He nodded. "Carbon monoxide is odorless and poisonous. Nasty stuff. Lars didn't know what he was breathing."

Her dad slept, still and helpless in the white-cloaked bed. A blue plastic hose protruded from his open mouth, extending to a large machine next to his bed. The machine inhaled and exhaled for him.

She thought of her father's ramblings. His confusion when she'd found him. He'd thought her mother was still alive.

Britt swallowed and tore her gaze from her father's still form. Although the doctor had cautioned that her father's recovery would take time, he'd assured Britt her dad was on the path out of the woods.

"News of tonight's big euchre tournament has been all over the TV and papers. Hell, I even saw an interview with your dad about it in the *Capitol Times.* Anyone who read it would have expected him to be gone most of the afternoon and night. That could only mean one thing." Mylinski leveled his hard, detective's stare on her. "Someone is trying to kill you, Britt."

A chill passed over her skin. She might as well tell Mylinski the whole story. "It's not the first time."

He leaned over her, his forehead furrowing. Worried but not surprised. "Want to 'fess up?"

"This morning a car tried to run me down."

A flush crept up Mylinski's neck. He shook his head as if disgusted. "And you're just telling me now? Didn't it occur to you to report this earlier? Or doesn't it bug you that someone wants you dead? Man, sometimes I think the guys downtown are right. You do have ice in your veins."

"I didn't take it seriously until now." Guilt twisted deep within her. Jack's warnings echoed in her mind. If she had listened to him, if she had been more careful, would her father be at home hunched over his police scanner instead of lying in this hospital bed?

No, she couldn't have done anything to prevent what had happened. She'd never have guessed someone would invade her home and sabotage her furnace. She'd never have imagined the desperation that would lead to such an attack. The only way she could have prevented the assault on her father was to die in that parking ramp.

She took a deep breath and told Mylinski the details she could remember. "Jack Alcott was with me. He might remember more."

Mylinski raised his eyebrows. "I'll have to ask him. He's sitting out in the corridor."

Britt straightened in her chair. A flutter worked its way through her arms and legs and settled in her chest. She glanced at the clock over her father's bed. Midnight, and Jack waited in the hospital. She could still feel the warmth of his fingers tracing her cheekbone.

His touch had transported her through time. The memories, the passion.

The deception.

The flutter in her chest died. He hid a secret. A secret she hadn't been able to ask her father to divulge. Swallowing, she peered up at Mylinski, the fluorescent lights stinging her eyes. She had to get her mind back on track. "What have you found on the case?"

Mylinski sighed and leaned against the wall. "Have you considered the attempt on your life in the parking ramp may be tied to Tangi Rowe's homicide investigation?"

Britt slumped back in the chair. Try as she might, she couldn't imagine any punk she'd prosecuted going to these lengths for revenge. No, she was a threat to someone. Someone with the means to rent a car and the know-how to sabotage a furnace. "There could be a connection to Tangi's death."

Mylinski nodded. "That's how we're going to approach it. You can't go home tonight. I booked you a room in the new budget hotel down the street.''

Britt nodded.

''I'll arrange for an officer to keep an eye on you.''

She nodded again. The weight of fear and anger bore down on her shoulders until she wanted to cry out. Someone was trying to kill her. Someone had almost succeeded in killing her father.

She couldn't dwell on this. She had to get her mind on something else. Images of Jack's haunted face and dark eyes popped into her mind. She pushed them away. The investigation. She'd focus on Tangi's murder investigation. ''Did Spinnetti's prints come back from the lab?''

Mylinski grunted and pulled a piece of candy from his pocket. ''They didn't match. We had to let him go.''

Alarm jolted through her like an electrical charge. Spinnetti's bulldog build and doberman snarl flashed through her mind. The man was capable of murder. Of this she had no doubt. ''You don't think Spinnetti—''

''Nope. It wasn't Spinnetti who sabotaged your furnace. We let him go, we didn't forget him. He's been under surveillance since he hit the street. He's been a good boy the whole time.''

''Then who do you think did it?'' Britt had ideas of her own, but she wanted Mylinski's take.

''My money is on an Alcott. Any Alcott.''

''Except Jack.'' As soon as the words left her mouth, she wanted to bite them back. She didn't want Mylinski to guess the conflict raging inside her.

He nodded, his eyebrows raising again in that knowing look. ''Except Jack.''

Too late. He knew.

"Al, would you mind asking the nurse for a glass of water? I'm thirsty."

He eyed her suspiciously, but left to do as she asked.

As soon as he stepped out, Britt slumped back in her chair. She wasn't thirsty at all. She needed to be alone. She needed to think.

Keeping her mind off Jack was impossible. Everywhere she looked, she saw his face. Every train of thought led back to him. Raising her hand to her face, she traced the path Jack's fingers had taken over her cheek.

Ever since Jack had strolled into her office with Grant, her emotions had woven like a drunkard walking a chalk line. Both bitterness and longing swirled inside her, so jumbled she couldn't sort one from the other. She'd stumbled off the line all right. She just didn't know on which side she'd fallen.

Either way, she could no longer keep her head clear. She had to put the past on hold. Later she could wrestle with the betrayal, the secrets, the longing. Now she needed emotional distance. From the past. From the bitterness. From Jack.

BY THE TIME Britt kissed her dad's forehead and left his room, the first light of dawn glimmered through a window at the end of the corridor. The day from hell had ended. She'd crossed into tomorrow. And things would be different.

She'd return to her old self, the passionless, single-minded assistant district attorney that Mylinski liked to joke about. She'd regain control over her life. And she'd slam Tangi's killer behind bars.

But not without several hours of sleep first.

She turned the corner and strode out of the ICU. Halfway down the corridor, she saw him.

Slumped in a chair near the elevator, Jack slept, his suit rumpled, a lock of sable hair flopped over his forehead.

Britt swallowed into a dry throat. She stopped and stood in the middle of the long hall, her arms hanging limp at her sides.

Jack didn't move. The elevator door stood open just behind him.

The last thing she wanted was to have to deal with Jack right now. Just the sight of him threatened to dismantle her control. Maybe she could sneak past without waking him. She started for the elevator, tiptoeing on the balls of her feet to prevent her heels from sounding on the floor.

Her pulse fluttered in her ears. She drew even with him. A few more steps and she'd be in the elevator.

He stirred and opened a dark eye. "Britt."

For a moment, her heart lodged in her throat, then fell to somewhere in the vicinity of her toes. She forced ice into her voice and gaze. "Jack."

He stood, stretching his long legs and working the cricks from his neck. "How's Lars doing?"

His sleep-roughened voice stirred ghosts deep inside her. Images of whispered passion and bare skin. She swallowed again. She couldn't allow herself to respond to the raspy sensuality in his voice, the caring in his words.

"He's doing as well as can be expected. Thanks for your concern." Tearing her gaze from Jack, she hurried toward the elevator. She charged through the open door and punched the lobby button.

He slid in beside her, and the door closed.

Designed to carry hospital gurneys, the elevator was plenty large. But the walls seemed to close around her the moment Jack stepped inside. His scent filled the small space, leather and musk. His heat penetrated her tired bones. She didn't dare speak. Eyes glued to the numbers over the door, she stood very still and gulped air.

"Do you have a place to stay?" His deep voice cut the silence.

"Detective Mylinski booked me a room at the new budget hotel. The police are going to keep an eye on me there."

He nodded, his gaze traveling over her face and neck in a gentle caress.

Her skin tingled as if his fingers did the stroking. She kept her eyes focused on the flashing numbers. This had to be the slowest elevator in Madison.

"I'll drive you."

Her throat closed. The thought of being trapped with him in the confines of his Jaguar was too much. She shook her head. "I'll call a cab."

The elevator door opened and she bolted for the open lobby.

But he clutched her elbow before she broke clear of the door. "Don't be ridiculous. I have my car here. And in case you've forgotten, someone out there wants you dead."

Of course she hadn't forgotten. It wasn't the sort of thing one forgets. But with her control over her emotions tenuous at best, maybe death was preferable to crawling into Jack's Jaguar with him. Alone. "A cab will be perfectly safe."

He frowned, eyebrows turning down, eyes dark

with irritation. He loomed over her, his broad chest nearly touching her breasts. If she inhaled deeply, she'd press against his hard body. "Forget about the cab, Britt. You're coming with me."

Weakness assaulted her knees. Her head swam. She was tired. So tired. What did it matter if he drove her to the hotel? Fighting him would cost her more energy than just enduring the five-minute drive. And she was lacking in the energy department. "Fine. You can drop me off. Now step back."

He stood firm, staring down at her until she thought she would scream. He cocked a dark brow. "This is ridiculous. What do you think I'm going to do to you?"

What *did* she think he'd do? Take her in his arms? Kiss her the way he used to? Make her feel again?

He was right. She was being ridiculous. All she needed was a few hours' sleep. Then she could cope. Then she could regain control of her emotions, her life. Then she could focus on Tangi's murder.

She cleared her throat, forcing as much ire into her voice as she could. "I'm tired. Lead the way, or I'm calling that cab."

Jack turned and walked toward the parking ramp exit.

Britt followed at a safe distance. A short drive, and she'd be free of him. Then she could shove the memories aside and regain her perspective.

Their footsteps echoed, loud as gunshots, through the dead-quiet parking structure. Jack's car sat alone under a bright light, its sleek British-racing-green body a copy of the Jaguar he'd owned five years ago.

She focused on her shoes and the stained concrete

beneath. Five minutes. Five minutes and she'd be free of Jack. Free of the past. At least for a while.

He opened the door and she climbed inside. Settling in the seat, she reached across to open the driver's door for Jack.

He circled the car, his fluid stride reflecting in the rearview mirror. He settled into the seat next to her, a grin spreading across his lips. "Thanks for opening the door."

Britt leaned back in her seat and fastened her seat belt. Terrific. She'd fallen so easily into patterns of the past. She hadn't given it a second thought.

He started the car and pulled out of the ramp, the engine purring like a contented lover.

Except for the orange blush to the east, the sun still hid behind the horizon. Streetlights glittered in the cold dawn. Patterns of light and dark moved through the car, casting Jack's face in alternating highlight and shadow.

Somewhere a half-dozen sirens screamed. She focused on the sound, painful and shrill. Another tragedy. Another person transported to the hospital. Or to the morgue. Thank God, disaster was sparse in Madison, Wisconsin. She couldn't deal with the glut of anguish in a city the size of Chicago.

She held on to the thought, in a futile attempt to keep her mind from wandering to the man at the wheel. His nearness spurred her racing pulse. His cologne mingled with the aroma of the car's leather. A heady fog settled in Britt's tired brain.

Jack glanced at her out of the corner of his eye. "I think by now we can assume these attempts on your life are related to Tangi's murder."

Britt nodded. Had Jack also identified members of

his own family as suspects? "Who do you think wants me dead?"

The planes of his face seemed stark in the cold glare of the streetlights. "The person responsible for Tangi's death. Or someone trying to protect him or her."

"Are you willing to admit that Grant or another member of your family might be responsible?"

A muscle tightened along his jawline. "I didn't say anything like that."

"But it has occurred to you, hasn't it?"

His pained expression testified that it had.

"Face it, Jack, if Grant killed Tangi, chances are he's the one trying to kill me. He left the restaurant early, remember? He could have waited for me in the parking ramp. He could have gone to my house later to sabotage my furnace."

Jack shook his head. "I still don't see it. Not Grant."

"Why not Grant?"

"Can you imagine Grant slinking around your basement, tinkering with your furnace? He doesn't have the creativity or the initiative. Besides, I know he didn't kill Tangi. You saw him. Her death crushed him. He's not that good an actor."

Britt frowned. Jack could believe whatever he wanted. No matter what he said, he couldn't convince her of Grant's innocence. But she was open to Jack's theory of the crime. "If not Grant, then who?"

"I shouldn't be talking about this."

"No, you shouldn't. Why are you talking about it? Trying to throw my investigation off track?"

The lines framing his eyes deepened. He squinted into oncoming headlights. "Because I think you should protect yourself, damn it. You've got to take these attempts on your life seriously.''

''And what makes you think I'm not?''

''A hotel room with no security is not serious.''

She shook her head with frustration. Apparently a single police officer wasn't enough security for Mr. Jackson Alcott. He'd probably insist the entire force be posted outside her door. She glared at him. No point in wasting her breath arguing. ''Who else do you suspect wants me dead?''

''Anyone who might have killed Tangi.''

''Like who?''

''Tia, for instance.''

Britt nodded. Tia was her second favorite suspect. Tia's alibi relied on Grant and vice-versa. One could easily be lying to protect the other. ''Why do *you* think Tia might be responsible?''

''Tia wants a baby. She's been trying to get pregnant for years. Can you imagine how news of Tangi's pregnancy hit her?''

Britt could imagine. The shock. The betrayal. The anger. She could imagine the emotions all too well. ''But if she was angry enough to kill Tangi, wouldn't she be angry enough to let Grant take the fall for her murder? Why would she lie to provide him with an alibi?''

''I'm not saying the alibi is a lie. But remember, we're talking about Tia here. Being a congressman's wife is everything to her. And she'll lose everything if you charge Grant with murder. That's enough reason to lie. And enough reason to try to kill you.''

Britt nodded. He was right again. ''With all the work she's done with low-income housing, she might know her way around a furnace.''

"Exactly."

"Who else?"

The sharp planes of Jack's face grew rigid. "Roger."

Roger. The man would go to any lengths to protect his chosen son. "Possible. But he had an alibi for the night of Tangi's death. He was with your mother all night. Anyway, I *really* can't see Roger slinking around my basement."

"He wouldn't do it himself. He'd pay someone. And he's ruthless enough to do it. More ruthless than you know."

When it came to Roger's ruthlessness, she had no problem believing Jack. She could still see the twisted smile on Roger's face when Jack pulled her from his study. Roger Alcott wouldn't have any qualms about killing her. Or Tangi. She'd bet her life on it.

Jack swung the car to the right at a flashing yellow stoplight. The Jaguar hugged the corner—the wrong corner.

He had turned the wrong way.

Britt jolted straight in her seat. "Where are you taking me?"

Shadow cloaked his face, hiding his expression. "You were almost killed. And not just once. I'm not taking any chances."

Panic prickled along the back of her neck. He couldn't be suggesting he protect her himself. Could he? "The police will check on me at the hotel, Jack. I'll be fine."

"My condo is more secure than any hotel."

"Your condo?" Memories circled the edge of her mind like vultures hungry to pick at the carcass of her self-control. She couldn't sit in his living room, eat in his kitchen, sleep in his—"I'm not staying with you, Jack."

"You can call your detective and let him know where you are."

"No." To her horror, instead of ringing with conviction, the word sounded like a breathless question.

"I'm making sure you're safe."

Full-blown panic squeezed her chest. She gripped the armrest until her fingers ached. "You're making sure I'm safe? What a laugh. The only time I'm *not* safe is when I'm with you. The only person who can hurt me is you."

She choked on the last few words. Dizziness swept over her. She couldn't believe she'd said that to him. To him. She'd laid her fears bare. She'd shown him her Achilles heel and helped him aim the arrow.

"The only one who *can* protect you is me."

"Your ego is amazing. I hate to break this to you, but I don't need you, Jack. The police—"

"An hourly drive past the hotel isn't good enough. The police can't protect you like I can." His nostrils flared like an angry bull's.

"You mean the police won't lie to me? They won't keep secrets from me? They won't treat me like a child?"

Jack grimaced. "I live on the top floor of a security-locked building. I can screen the lobby visually thanks to a security camera, and I can lock the elevator so it doesn't open on my floor. Even someone with a key can't get in if I don't want them to. I can sure as hell protect you better than an overworked police force."

Resentment burned in the pit of Britt's stomach. He refused to address her father's secret, yet he had appointed himself her guardian. "If you think I'm going to stay with you, you're—"

"The guest bedroom has its own bath. You'll have all the privacy you could want."

"That's not the point, Jack." She couldn't stay anywhere near him, let alone in his condominium. *That* was the point.

The Jaguar crested a hill and the lake's flame-kissed waves surged in front of them. A brick building jutted five stories tall on the edge of the water. Architecture from a past age among the adjacent modern cement structures.

A shiver claimed her. She'd heard Jack had purchased the penthouse condo after he'd broken their engagement. She'd avoided this street, this whole section of town, for five years. She'd give anything to avoid it a little longer. "Jack, I—"

"We'll talk about it inside." He punched the button of a remote under the dashboard, and the underground garage door lifted.

"We have no reason to talk."

"Then don't talk. I don't care. But we *are* going inside." Jack piloted the Jaguar into the garage. The door lowered behind them like a stone rolling across the mouth of a tomb.

He pulled the car into a parking space and turned off the ignition. He got out of the car, circled behind, and opened her door. "Coming?"

She'd faced all the ghosts she cared to in the past twenty-four hours. She couldn't endure any more. She stayed planted in the seat.

He shrugged. "You can stay in the car if you want, but my guest room is much more comfortable."

She didn't move a muscle.

His eyebrows plunged into a frown. "Come on. You can call your detective."

Mylinski. Yes, she had to call Mylinski. If the squad car checked the hotel and she wasn't there, Al would have half the force out searching for her. She glanced at the car's dashboard. "I'll use your cell phone."

Jack's frown deepened. "No, you won't."

"Why not?"

"I won't let you."

Anger flashed through her. Strength surged to her leaden limbs. Embracing her wrath, she nurtured it until it blossomed inside her. Her head cleared. Logic, cold and bitter, soothed her trembling insides. As long as she stayed angry, she could shove aside the past, the memories.

And she could keep her perspective long enough to call Mylinski and demand he send a squad car to pick her up. "Fine. I'll come in to use your phone. But don't bother making up the bed in your guest room. I won't be staying."

Jack held his hands in front of him, palms up. "If your detective agrees to give you twenty-four-hour protection, you can leave with my blessing."

"I don't need your blessing, Jack. In some states, kidnapping is punishable by the death penalty."

"Unfortunately for you, Wisconsin doesn't have the death penalty." He grinned and held out his hand to her.

Ignoring his hand, she climbed out of the car. She followed him into the elevator, like a convict who has run out of appeals trudging to the electric chair.

The tiny elevator seemed to pulsate with Jack's energy, vitality. Gnawing her bottom lip, she riveted her gaze on the numbers above the door. One...Two... The sleeve of his coat brushed her own, a sound like the rustling of rumpled sheets. Britt clamped down on her lip until pain warned her to stop. Three...Four...

Finally, the door slid open on the fifth floor. She followed Jack into a simple, elegant entry hall, her heels resounding on the parquet floor.

The hall opened into a large room filled with simple contemporary furniture and enclosed by windows rather than walls. Beyond the windows was a patio. And beyond the patio, the focal point of the room sparkled in the brightening rays of dawn.

Even from the height of the fifth floor, Lake Mendota's undulating waves seemed to lap at her shield of anger, filling her with heat and the awareness of Jack beside her.

He nodded toward the water. "That's why I bought this place. During a big case, my life can get pretty crazy. When I'm about to lose my mind, I come back to Madison and stare at the lake. It helps me get things back in perspective."

Perspective. That was what Britt needed right now. But the relentless surge and release of the waves wasn't helping her. Not one bit.

Jack strode to the patio door and peered out. His suit coat, though rumpled, fit his wide shoulders and narrow waist with the sensual grace reserved for a man's own skin. Or was she remembering the countless times she'd watched him like this in the past? Those times, he'd been naked.

She tore her eyes away. "Where's your phone?"

He gestured in the direction of the kitchen with the sweep of his hand.

She stumbled across the room, grateful to be away

from his heat and the restless swell of the waves. She located the phone on the butcher block and punched in Mylinski's pager number. He called back within thirty seconds, and she explained the situation.

"I know the place," Mylinski said, his voice groggy with sleep. "And he's right. You'll be a lot safer there. I'll take care of the rest." He hung up before a protest could form on her lips.

She was stuck. Trapped in Jack's condo. The past staring her in the face. Teasing her. Tempting her.

She drew herself to her full height and thrust her chin forward. Just because she had to stay in Jack's condo didn't mean she had to sit with him, talk to him. She'd find the guest room and lock herself inside. She exited the kitchen and glanced around for a hallway that might lead to the guest room.

A large colorful poster caught her eye. Propped on a mahogany easel, the poster depicted scenes of cowboy round-ups and cowboys sleeping under the stars. A headline slashed across the top. Bonanza Boys' Ranch. Her heart syncopated its beat.

The ranch. He'd built the ranch. And from the towering pine trees, rolling hills and rock faces in the poster's photographs, he'd chosen the spot where he'd proposed to her so long ago.

A tingle stole up her spine, and she knew Jack stood behind her. "You built it. You went ahead and built it."

"I'm surprised you hadn't heard."

She wasn't surprised. Whenever she'd spotted his name in a *State Journal* article, she'd thrown the paper away. Except for stumbling upon a newscast here and there, she'd avoided learning what he was up to. Reminders had hurt too much.

He stepped closer, too close, his body heat igniting a hot flush in her cheeks.

She groped in her mind, trying to grab hold of the anger, the bitterness she'd felt at Jack's betrayal. All she grasped were memories of Jack's tongue exploring her mouth, their sweat-slick bodies on a summer night, his scent clinging to her sheets after they'd made love.

"I have blueprints of the ranch and photos of the construction if you'd like to see them. I wanted to send them to you. After all, you were in on the project from the very beginning. But I didn't know how you'd react."

She knew how she'd react. She'd have thrown the unopened envelope away, just like the newspapers. Just like she'd tried so hard to discard the memories.

He rested his hand on her shoulder, turning her to face him. His eyes consumed her, dark and fiery as hot coals. "I'll show them to you. Better late than never."

Memories flooded her mind. The days exploring pine forests, the nights exploring each other. And now he was right in front of her again. And so close. Close enough to touch. To kiss. To love.

No.

She couldn't think. She couldn't breathe. She jolted away from him and bolted for the patio door.

Once outside, she concentrated on breathing. In and out. In and out. Leaning against the wrought-iron railing, she listened to the waves crash five stories below. She'd be damned if she'd give in to the memories. She'd be damned.

The patio door opened and closed. His footsteps echoed off concrete and brick. He came up close be-

hind her, the whisper of his breath teasing her ear.
"Britt, we have to talk."

The resonance of his voice shook her to the core.
Her head whirled with his masculine scent. She
groped for the anger that had saved her earlier. "Like
I said before, unless you're planning to tell me everything, we have nothing to talk about."

"Britt, look at me."

She turned around, pressing the small of her back
against the cold railing.

Taut muscles twitched in his jaw. "I was trying to
protect you. I would never have walked away from
you otherwise. I want you to know that."

"It doesn't matter, Jack."

"How can you say that? Of course it matters. Under other circumstances, I never would have left you.
But under *these* circumstances, I chose the lesser of
two evils."

Britt wrapped her arms around her middle. He'd
kept the secret to protect her. From his father's threat
to destroy her career. From the secret he wouldn't tell.
He'd believed the truth would devastate her more than
his betrayal.

But did all the reasons on earth make a difference?
Wasn't he doing the same thing her mother had done?
And Tangi? And apparently her father? "You mean,
you didn't trust I could handle the truth."

He raised a hand to brush hair from her forehead.
"I couldn't live with the idea of hurting you."

The feathery wisp of his touch sent shudders skit-
tering along her nerves. She clenched her fists.
"That's funny, Jack, because you hurt me. You hurt
me badly."

"I know." His voice barely rose above a whisper.

He traced a finger along her cheekbone. "I'm sorry. But I'd do it again. Roger gave me an ultimatum. I know Roger. He would have made good on his threats."

"Maybe you should have known *me* well enough to tell me the truth."

Pain shone from his eyes as clearly as if she'd sucker-punched him in the gut. "I do know you, Britt. That's why keeping this secret from you tears me apart."

She shuddered at the intimacy in his voice. She didn't want to hear this. He wasn't going to tell her father's secret. And she couldn't swallow his apologies. Or his explanations. "I want to be alone."

"I love you, Britt. I always have. That's why I had to walk away. That's why I need to protect you now."

Love.

Her head whirled.

Love.

She wanted to scream. She wanted to pound her fists against his chest. But her voice and hands wouldn't obey.

Memories clamored inside her, struggling to take over. She remembered it all, everything about him. The scratch of his whiskers when he nuzzled her breasts after a night of passion. The hot surge of him when they joined. The fierce love in his voice when he cried out her name. She had once loved Jack. With all her heart, mind, and soul. But that was in the past. Along with the secrets, the betrayal.

She wouldn't let him drag her back to the past. She couldn't.

"You're so beautiful," he muttered under his breath.

Panic rasped in her ears. She needed space. Distance. "Jack, please."

He cupped his hands around her neck. Running his thumbs along her jaw, he tilted her head back. Hunger mixed with the darkness of his eyes. He lowered his mouth to hers.

His kiss burned fierce and hot.

Longing overcame her. She leaned into him, responding to each demanding stroke of his lips as if there were no past, no future. Only now. She wrapped her arms around his neck. Opening her mouth, she invited him inside.

He deepened his kiss, compelling her to match him stroke for stroke, joust for joust.

She rose to his challenge. Her heart beat savagely in her rib cage. Her breasts pressed against the hard muscle of his chest. Her nipples hardened to throbbing points, straining against the imprisoning lace of her bra.

God, she wanted him. She craved him.

A moan of desire caught in her throat. How had she lived without him? Oh God, how could she continue living without him now that she'd found him again?

Pain and fear pulsed inside her, keeping time with the drumming of her heart. The pain of all she'd lost. The fear of all she had yet to lose.

She pulled back from him, the wrought-iron railing digging into her spine. She couldn't allow herself to give in to her longing. As much as she wanted to, she couldn't—they couldn't—go back to the way things used to be. Too much had been said.

And far too much had *not* been said.

"Jack. No. I can't do this." Her voice hovered in her ears, husky with wanting.

He raised an eyebrow. "Why not?"

Inhaling deeply, she raised her chin and met his eyes. "The truth, Jack. I need the truth."

Chapter Ten

Jack stepped back from Britt. Cold wind rushed to fill the void where the warmth of his body had been.

She closed her eyes and leaned against the cold patio railing, the crash of the waves echoing in her ears.

Her lips throbbed with the imprint of his. Her whole body ached for his touch. How she wished she could go back in time, before the hurt, before the betrayal, before the secrets. Back when Tangi was alive, and her mother was alive, and her father still carried his badge. Back when she loved Jack with all her heart.

But she could never go back. And she couldn't hide.

She opened her eyes and squinted into the rising sun. ''Tell me the secret, Jack. Tell me what Roger held over your head five years ago.''

A muscle along his jawline twitched. ''Like I said before, it's not my secret to tell. Lars has to be the one to tell you.''

''My father is in Intensive Care with a hose down his throat and a machine breathing for him.'' She stepped toward him, closing the gap. "Tell me, Jack."

Jack narrowed his eyes and tightened his mouth into a thin line. "I can't, Britt."

"You can't, or you won't?"

"I can't hurt you. I won't hurt you any more."

She gritted her teeth until they ached. Why couldn't she make him see? Why couldn't she make him understand? "You're hurting me more by not telling me."

He shook his head, staring past her and out at the waves. Lines etched the corners of his eyes and mouth, the stress of a secret he wouldn't share.

"You can't protect me from the truth, Jack. I'm going to find out eventually."

He looked straight at her. "Not from me."

Britt bit back a curse. She wanted to shake him. She wanted to pound some sense into him. How dare he decide what she should know and what she shouldn't? How dare he play God with her life?

She balled her hands into fists and met his eyes. What she saw stopped her dead.

Worry…caring…

Love.

He wanted to keep her from getting hurt. He still cared about her. Still loved her.

She let her hands drop limp by her sides. How could she make him see where she was coming from? How could she make him feel what she felt?

She could tell him. Explain to him how this secret tormented her. And how the truth would set her free.

She reached for him, his arm hard as marble under her hand. "Three years ago, my mother kept her cancer secret from me. Now, every day of this last week,

I've learned a new secret about Tangi's life. And on top of that, you tell me my dad is hiding something too. I don't know what or who to believe anymore. I feel like I'm going crazy. I need someone to be honest with me, Jack.'' Squeezing his arm, she drew him closer. ''I'm relying on you.''

Brooding darkness passed over his face like a shadow. He spun on his heel and walked away from her, pacing the length of the patio. When he turned back to face her, his dark eyes drilled into hers. Anguished. Tortured.

The wind's chill infiltrated her heart. He wasn't going to tell her. Even after she bared her soul to him, he couldn't bring himself to trust her with the truth. Despair, harsh and oppressive, threatened to strangle her.

No. She couldn't give in. She couldn't give up. She had to know.

And damn it, she'd find someone who'd tell her. If not her father, if not Jack, she'd find someone else. Someone who wasn't concerned with protecting her. Someone who would like nothing better than to cause her pain.

And she knew just the someone.

She glanced at the sun, now bright in the sky. ''What time does Roger receive visitors on a Saturday morning?''

Five giant strides and Jack stood next to her, a tight grip on her elbow as if he planned to physically detain her. ''Stay away from Roger.''

''Roger will tell me the truth.''

''Roger will do anything that suits his purpose.''

''The truth suits *my* purpose, Jack.'' The thought of facing Roger, pleading with him for the truth, turned her stomach. But in order to learn her father's secret, she'd fall to her knees in front of Satan himself. She swallowed her fear and raised her chin another notch. If Jack thought she was bluffing, he was mistaken. "I have to get on with the rest of my life. Now let go of me."

He didn't let go.

"You have a choice to make. You either protect me from the truth, or you protect me from Roger. You can't do both."

Jack frowned, pain and frustration shining in his eyes. He exhaled, a shuddering sigh of defeat. "You have no idea what you're asking."

Foreboding traveled over her skin like the prick of a thousand tiny needles. "Believe me, Jack. I know."

"I hope so." Eyes darkening with misery, he let his hand drop from her elbow.

She knew he'd relent. To Jack, anything was better than the notion of her submitting to Roger, allowing herself to be a target for his father's special brand of cruelty. He'd spent all his life protecting his mother, his sister, and even Grant from his father's ruthless manipulations. He'd spent his career protecting individuals from the big, bad government. He wouldn't come up short when it came to protecting her.

She braced herself. She'd wanted the truth and now she was about to get it. She hoped to God she could handle it.

"Roger cornered me the night of the party and ordered me to end our engagement. If I didn't call the wedding off, he promised to ruin your career and send your father to jail."

"What?" The cold wind pummeled her, driving a chill into her core. She shook her head. "What for?"

Jack held up a hand to silence her. He sucked in a breath like a jury foreman preparing to deliver the verdict. "Your father accepted bribes, Britt. Bribes that Roger's business associates paid him."

She bit the inside of her cheek. The coppery tang of blood tinged her mouth, but she couldn't feel any pain. She couldn't feel anything at all. "My father is an honest man. An honest cop."

"I didn't believe it either at first. But Roger has evidence to prove his allegations. I've seen cash transfers. I've seen bank records. The dates your father received large sums of money correspond to crucial mistakes he and his partner made investigating important cases. Cases that had to be dropped."

"It could be coincidence. You don't know where that money came from. He could have saved it. He could have won it betting with his friends on a Packer game. You're a defense attorney. You know damn well that without corroborating evidence, a cash transfer near the date of an alleged crime doesn't prove anything."

"I got corroboration before I pulled you aside at our engagement party. I talked to your father."

The crash of the waves grew deafeningly loud. She shook her head to clear away the sound. "What did my father say? Did he give you an explanation?"

"He admitted it was true, Britt."

No. Dread hummed in her ears, nearly drowning out Jack's words.

"It started out small. He kept one of Rico Gianni's trucks from being impounded during a small-time smuggling investigation. Then Gianni asked him to do more favors for him and for some of his pals.

When your father wanted out, one of Gianni's shadier business associates hired Jimmy Surles.''

Jimmy Surles. His name settled over her like a foul smell. She'd never forget the man who with one squeeze of the trigger, stole the life from her father's legs and the spirit from his eyes.

''What's Roger's role in all this?''

''He's walked the line, but it seems he's not involved in anything illegal. I've had him investigated. More than once. And except for his legitimate business dealings with Gianni, I've found nothing to tie him to any of it.''

She couldn't think. Numbness cloaked her like the heavy folds of a judge's black robes. It all fit together like a tidy little jigsaw puzzle. The bullet shot by Surles. Her father's hatred for the Alcotts.

Roger's words at their last meeting rang in her memory. *Have you ever wondered how a cop could save enough money to send his daughter to law school?*

At the D.A.'s office, they had a word for evidence that aligned this nicely. *Conviction.*

''Britt.''

She couldn't look at Jack. Instead, she focused on the waves and waited for the numbness to give way to pain. Her dad had taken bribes. Her dad. Bribes from Rico Gianni.

She inhaled deeply. Her life, her illusions crumbled to dust. All she could do was stand and listen to the crash of the waves. She'd insisted on the truth. She'd gotten it. Now she had to figure out a way to deal with it. She forced herself to meet Jack's eyes. ''I have to talk to my father. Maybe he can explain.''

''Do what you have to do.''

"If Dad says he didn't take bribes, I'm going to take his word."

Her father's word. Could she trust her father's word?

Betrayal stung like the jagged gash of broken glass. Though every cell in her being wanted to scream her dad's innocence, she knew Jack spoke the truth. Her father had sold out everything he believed in. Everything *she* believed in.

All her life she'd had a moral base, a foundation built by her parents' love and their belief in doing the right thing. The moral thing. Now, with a few words, her foundation lay in rubble at her feet. She was alone. No foundation. No base. No strength.

A tear trickled down her cheek.

Jack raised a hand to her cheek and wiped the tear away, his fingertips grazing her skin in a gentle caress. "I'm sorry, Britt. I knew what this would do to you."

Conflicted emotions swirled in her mind, making her dizzy. Now that she knew what her father had done, her life would never be the same. She could never go back. She understood that. She accepted that. But could she go forward? And could she ever bring herself to forgive him? And what about prison? Would Roger follow up on his threat and turn his evidence over to the police?

She didn't know. But it didn't matter. Not now. Now the only thing that meant a damn was the empty agony inside her.

Jack slipped an arm around her shoulder, pulling her against his warmth.

She leaned into him, drawing on his strength. She needed him. Now more than ever. Needed him to hold her. Needed him to love her. Needed him to convince her she wasn't alone in the world. "Jack, I…"

"Shhh." He gazed down at her, his eyes bright with understanding. With passion. "God, I've missed you, Britt."

She closed her eyes, relishing the hard press of his body. She wasn't alone. Jack was here. Jack was with her.

With a gentle pull, he untied the satin ribbon securing her hair and dropped it to the ground. Her hair fell loose, cloaking her shoulders. Burying a hand in it, he lowered his head and claimed her lips.

Circling her arms around his neck, she pulled him closer.

He deepened the kiss.

She fitted her body to his and plunged her fingers through his hair. Dark and silky, it flowed between her fingers like rain after a long drought. She drank him in. His leather and musk scent. The rough stubble covering his chin. The hard strength of his body. She wanted to be close to him. Needed to be close. Skin to skin. Soul to soul.

She worked a hand between them, tearing at the buttons of his shirt with her fingers.

He followed her lead. Her suit jacket hit the patio. He unbuttoned her blouse, freeing her from its confines. Drawing back, he left her lips aching for his, her fingers reaching for him.

The wind, cool and refreshing, caressed her, raising goose bumps over her chest and bare midriff. Her nipples throbbed against the lace of her bra. She wanted it off. She wanted nothing between them, not even a scrap of lace.

"Are you cold?"

God, no. She was burning up. Unable to find her voice, she shook her head.

He smiled and pushed the silky blouse off her shoulders. "Are you sure?"

"I'm hot as Hades." She straightened her arms by her sides. Her blouse fell in a puddle on the patio.

"I guess so."

His smile widened. He circled her with his arms and unhooked her bra. It went the way of her blouse.

Her breasts hung free, heavy with desire.

Jack drew in a sharp breath. He reached for her, his fingertips tracing each hardened nipple before cupping her breasts in his strong, warm hands. "God, you are beautiful. You are so beautiful."

Britt struggled to breathe, gulping in his scent.

He lowered his head, his lips and tongue tracing each nipple the way his fingers had.

Razor stubble scraped sensitive skin. Shivers splintered over her. This was no memory. As much as she'd wanted Jack five years ago, she wanted him more now.

He clasped her hand and led her inside. To his bedroom. To his bed. Once there, he continued to undress her. Piece by piece, each article of clothing fell to the floor. Her silky skirt, her nylon hose, and lastly, her lacy panties.

Eyeing her body, he moaned with appreciation.

Heat infused every place his gaze touched. Her nipples throbbed with the want of his kisses. Her core contracted with an emptiness she craved him to fill.

He ran his hands over her skin, tracing the path his gaze had forged. Then clutching her bottom with both hands, he pulled her against him.

She rocked against the length of his body, against his hard arousal. Desire coiled inside her.

He groaned, his fingers kneading her buttocks.

She wanted to fuse with him, join with him, never to be ripped apart. She wanted to touch him, taste him, no barriers between them.

She pulled back from him, fumbling with the remaining buttons on his shirt. She brushed her fingers over the soft dark hair sprinkling his chest.

He grabbed her wrists in both hands and guided her down on the soft bed. "Let me look at you. I want to feast my eyes on you."

She stretched across the huge bed, luxuriating in the ecstacy of his hungry gaze.

He slipped the white shirt off his shoulders and let it fall to the floor, his focus never straying from her breasts, her belly.

She parted her thighs and lay before him, exposed, vulnerable, drinking in the sight of his body the way he drank in hers. Never had she experienced such a surge of strength, of belonging.

He moved his fingers to his waist with greater urgency, unbuckling his belt, unzipping his fly. His trousers fell to the floor, revealing tight briefs and the bulge of his desire.

Her fingers itched to strip off those briefs. To see him. To hold him. To accept him into her body.

He hooked his thumbs in the elastic waistband.

"Wait." Britt sat up on the edge of the bed and slid her fingers between the elastic and his warm, smooth skin. Leaning forward, she littered kisses over his ridged stomach as she pushed the briefs down.

He sprang free, hard and vital. He wanted her.

And, oh God, did she want him.

Closing her hand around his length, she explored him as if for the first time. Touching, kissing, loving. Her desire fresh and new.

Then it was his turn again. A hand on each shoulder, he pressed her back down to the bed and covered her body with his. Starting with her earlobes, he drifted over her, leaving no part of her unkissed, no part uncaressed.

Delicious shivers danced over her skin. She wanted him inside her. Joined with her. Part of her. She never wanted to be alone again. "Jack..."

He seemed to know exactly what she wanted, what she needed, as if they were of one mind. He positioned himself above her. Claiming her lips with his, he eased into her.

She opened to receive him. To accept him. To join with him. Thrust for thrust. Need for need. Love for love.

His heartbeat vibrated through her chest and her own heart echoed the frantic rhythm. She wrapped her legs around him, bonding him to her. Her breath quickened. A plea sprang from her lips.

He worked his hand between their sweat slick bodies. Touching the center of her being, he sent her over the edge into a free fall of ecstacy.

Soon he joined her, crying out her name with such fierceness it brought tears to her eyes.

She lay quiet for a long time, body throbbing with fulfillment.

Breathing deep and regular, Jack dozed beside her, his scent embracing her, his warm breath caressing her neck. The lines around his eyes had vanished, the hard planes of his face softened. He was the Jack she knew, the idealistic, passionate Jack. The man who in court exhibited a lawyer's rapier wit and gnashing teeth, but who when alone with her, could be strong and vulnerable and comic and sincere. He was the man she used to love—the man she still loved.

And he was with her. She wasn't alone. With that knowledge, she could face any secret. Any truth. And she could do what she had to do.

Even give up her role in Tangi's murder investigation.

Distress stirred deep in the pit of her stomach. By making love with Jack, she had crossed the line. No, she'd erased the line completely. She'd made love to her prime suspect's attorney, and now she was neck-deep in conflict of interest.

She had a choice to make. Either she pretended this morning never happened. Or she requested Tangi's case be reassigned.

She knew the answer even before she glanced at Jack. She couldn't give him up. Not now that she'd found him again. She couldn't go back to being alone.

She scooched out from beneath his arm and stood, aching as if she'd just toured the country on horseback. With a glance back at his long legs tangled in the sheets, she made her way to the kitchen.

Spotting the cordless phone on the butcher block in the center of the kitchen, she picked it up. She'd still keep her promise to Tangi. She still wouldn't let Grant get away with murder. She'd still make him pay. She just wouldn't argue Tangi's case herself.

A walnut clock above the sink read noon. Dillon Reese always worked Saturdays. Hopefully, she'd catch him at the office before he left.

She entered the number, nerves jittering as if she'd just finished her second pot of coffee. Tangi's face flashed in her memory. She was doing the right thing, damn it. She was doing the only thing she could. She paced in a circle around the kitchen floor.

The phone rang once. Twice.

She paced faster, orbiting the butcher block and marching into the study. Outfitted as a home office, the room was complete with computer, law library, and fax machine spewing paper. Jack's connection with his law offices in Chicago, no doubt.

Three rings.

She stepped toward the bookshelf.

Four rings.

Her foot connected with something solid, sending her sprawling headfirst into the criminal statutes of Wisconsin.

She reached out to break her fall. The phone flew out of her hand, clattering against the side of the desk. Gritting her teeth with frustration, she glared down at the object that had tripped her.

A colorful tapestry tote bag lay on its side, the toe of a black men's dress shoe peeking out the top. Crumbs of dried red mud and fragments of oak leaves spilled onto the floor.

Her blood ran to ice.

Mylinski's report came back to her in excruciating detail. An oak forest. Footprints in the mud. The imprint of expensive dress shoes.

She was looking at evidence. Evidence of Tangi's murder.

Evidence in Jack's possession.

Doubt spiraled through her brain. Would Jack hinder the prosecution of a murder? Would he throw away his ticket to practice law? Would he risk everything to protect his brother? To protect his family?

Would Jack betray her?

Britt closed her eyes and waited for her dizziness to subside. Pain sliced through her chest as if a switchblade carved out her heart. She didn't know what to think, where to turn. She knew only one thing for certain.

She'd never felt so alone.

Chapter Eleven

The shrill bleat of a telephone sliced through Jack's dream.

No. Not now. Not when he was dreaming of Britt. Her long legs wrapped around him, the taste of her breasts, her softness and strength as she opened to him.

And it was no dream this time. She was here, with him, in his bed. Hunger stirring inside him, he reached for her.

His arm embraced nothing but pillow. Damn. Where was she? He shot fully awake, craning his neck to read the bedside clock. Nearly three o'clock in the afternoon. He'd slept the day away.

The phone rang again. He grabbed the receiver. "Yes."

"So, Jackson," Roger's voice boomed. "Looking for Britt?"

Jack glanced around his bedroom. Where was Britt? Silence hung thick in the air. No running water from the bathroom, no rustle of movement from the kitchen or living room. He paused a moment to collect his thoughts. "What do you want, Roger?"

"I thought you should know where that Gerritsen woman is."

"All right, I'll bite. Where is she?"

"She's here at the house with her storm troopers. And if your brain was in your head instead of in your pants, you'd be here protecting the rights of the family."

Jack sat up in bed, ripping the imprisoning sheets from around his legs. "Britt is *where?*"

"She's here. At the house, damn it. I suggest you get here and control her. Now." The phone went dead.

Jack threw down the receiver and bolted out of bed. What was going on? Just this morning Britt had driven him to ecstacy and beyond. And now she was at the house? What the hell had happened while he'd been sleeping?

He stumbled to the bathroom and ran a toothbrush across his teeth and a comb through his hair. After dousing his face with cold water and pulling on a pair of pants and a shirt, he grabbed his battery-powered razor and headed for the elevator.

A myriad of questions played through his mind. After what they'd shared, why had Britt sneaked out before he woke up? Why did she go to the house? She'd promised not to involve his mother and sister. She'd promised not to question the family further until after Kimberly's wedding. Why would she choose not to honor their deal?

Something must have happened, but what? He ransacked his brain for an explanation and came up with nothing. He didn't have any idea what was going on, but he'd damn well find out.

ROGER YANKED OPEN the front door the moment Jack's foot touched the landing. "She's upstairs."

Jack nodded to the police officer at the door and stepped into the foyer. "What's going on?"

"That Gerritsen woman is after the family, that's what's going on. Do something about it—now." Roger gestured with a crystal tumbler clutched in his trembling fist.

A police officer brushed past Jack and mounted the sweeping staircase. Grant's room. They were searching Grant's room.

"Did Britt show you a warrant?"

"Do you think I would let her bust in here without one? I can tell you one thing. The judge that signed that warrant will be lucky if he holds onto his job until the next election." He raised his glass in a bitter toast.

"Jackson? Is that you?" Jack's mother rushed into the foyer and collapsed into his arms. Frail as a china doll, she clung to him.

"Everything will be all right, Mother." Jack patted her thin back. He needed to find out what the hell was going on before he made such promises, but his mother's deathly pallor was enough to make him say anything to calm her down.

Roger tossed back the remainder of his whiskey. "You'd better take care of this situation, Jackson. Fitzroy, that damn poor excuse for a D.A., isn't taking my calls. If this goes any further, it's on your shoulders."

Jack's mother flinched at Roger's bellow. Tears trickled down her ashen cheeks. "Grant can't go to jail, Jackson. You can't let Britt do this."

Grant. That's who was missing from this happy family party. "Where *is* Grant?"

Jack's mother laid a fragile hand on his shoulder. "He's outside. By the lake. He couldn't take this. It's all very upsetting to him."

Figures. Leave it to Grant to migrate as far from the trauma as he could. "Don't worry about Grant, Mom. I'll take care of him."

His mother pulled back from his shoulder, her lower lip quivering. Lipstick smudged her chin like a bloody wound.

Pity flooded Jack's heart. Pity and fear. His mother couldn't take this kind of stress. She needed protection. Mimi Alcott had never been a strong woman.

Roger ignored his wife. "I don't want an arrest, Jackson. Once charges are brought, Grant's career is over. That woman is not going to ruin everything I've worked for."

Everything *he'd* worked for? Just like Roger to focus on how this situation would affect him. No thought for Grant's future or his own wife's health. The family existed to reflect glory on Roger. First, last and always.

Jack turned his attention back to his mother. He slipped an arm around her shoulders.

Roger waved a dismissive hand. "Mimi, go back into the living room and sit down. You look like hell."

Jack seethed at the way Roger treated his mother. He opened his mouth to protest.

Throwing him a final beseeching look, his mother tore away from his supportive grasp.

Since Jack could remember, Roger had always held Mimi under his thumb. She learned only what *he* thought she should know. Decided only what *he* thought she should decide, the way *he* thought she should decide it. The man was a tyrant, plain and simple. Jack would like nothing better than to see him reap the misery he'd sown over the years.

But not at Grant's expense. Or his mother's. He closed his mouth without saying anything and watched his mother retreat into the living room.

Roger jiggled his highball glass, ice chiming against crystal. "I'll be in my study tracking down the judge that signed that warrant. Let me know when you've set things straight." He spun on his heel and marched down the hall.

Through the arched doorway leading to the living room, Jack caught a glimpse of Kyle holding Kimberly. Kyle's calm, soothing tone hummed above Roger's retreating footsteps, his words unintelligible.

Jack caught Kyle's eye. With a wave of his hand, he motioned his future brother-in-law into the hall.

After giving Kimberly a quick kiss on the forehead, Kyle joined him. "Am I glad you're here, Jack."

"What is your take on this?"

Kyle tugged at the lobe of his ear. "To tell you the truth, I'm a little over my head here. I deal with financial records, profit-and-loss statements, computer crime. I don't know much about representing a murderer."

So much for his second chair. Just as he'd suspected, Kyle was worthless when it came to Grant's defense. But legal advice wasn't the kind of help Jack needed from Kyle. "My mother doesn't look good. Her heart can't take much more of this. Would you and Kimberly take her to the hospital?"

Kyle gave a sharp nod. A look of relief poured into his eyes. "Done."

Jack sighed. His sister's future husband may not be good at thinking for himself, but he knew how to follow orders. The perfect son-in-law for Roger. And after hearing Kyle's tender tone soothing Kimberly, Jack had to admit Kyle would probably be a pretty good husband for his sister, too.

Within seconds, Kyle escorted Kimberly and Mimi out the front door.

With his mother and Kimberly cared for and Roger sequestered in his study with his telephone, Jack started for the staircase. He needed to see Britt. Only Britt could tell him what was really going on.

He took the stairs two at a time.

Tia's slurred whining met him halfway up the stairs. She stood at the door to her suite, a goblet of blood-red wine in her hand. Ten-to-one, it wasn't her first glass of the day. Or even her first bottle. "You have no right to enter my room and rummage through my private things. This is harassment."

A balding detective leaned on the frame of the door, his bulk barring her entrance. Pulling a cellophane-wrapped candy from his pocket, he grinned at her. "Want one?"

Tia stamped her foot. "I want you out of my room."

The detective glanced down at the candy. "Suit yourself." He peeled off the cellophane and popped the morsel into his mouth. "Why don't you wait downstairs with the rest of the family?"

Tia squared her shoulders. "So it's easier on you?"

"So it's easier on everyone."

She tossed her cropped black head. "I'm calling my lawyer."

The detective glanced in Jack's direction. "Somebody must have beat you to it."

She whirled around, her dark eyes shining, her cheeks flushed with anger. "Jackson. You're here."

"Obviously." After fighting his way through the rest of the family, the last thing he wanted was to slug it out with Tia. "Do as the detective says, Tia. I'll take it from here."

Extending a red nail, she pointed at him. "You got Grant into this mess. If it wasn't for your deal with Britt Gerritsen, Grant would never have talked to her. And she wouldn't be here now, tearing up my life. I told you she wouldn't stick to your little deal. I told you. But you didn't want to see. Not where *she* was concerned." Tia gestured toward the bedroom with her glass, sending a wave of wine splashing onto the plush carpet.

Jack gritted his teeth. He'd had enough of Tia. More than enough. "Tia, go downstairs."

She moved closer to him, her wine-sweet breath fanning his face. "I hope she's good in bed, Jack. I hope she's good enough to justify selling out your family."

"Detective Mylinski, please escort Mrs. Alcott downstairs." The husky timbre of Britt's voice filled the doorway.

Tia planted her feet. "I'm not going anywhere."

Jack peered past her and into the bedroom suite.

Britt stared back at him, her eyes glinting as cold and hard as blue sapphires. Her high cheekbones and flawless skin carried all the human warmth of an alabaster sculpture.

Memory wafted through his mind like a summer breeze. The heat of her flushed skin, the flame in her eyes, the soul-deep passion they had shared just a few hours ago. Now all of it was gone. Nothing left but the deepening chill of winter.

The chill pierced his chest.

Britt raised her chin, her lush hair bound to her head by a barrette, her slender curves covered severely by a dark wool suit. "I may want to talk to you later, Tia. But for now, please wait downstairs."

A smile twisted Detective Mylinski's lips. Grabbing Tia's flailing arm, he muscled her past Jack. "Come now. Let's go downstairs and see if we can't get you a nice cup of coffee."

"Go to hell," Tia snarled at the detective.

"Already there, believe me." Mylinski escorted her down the hall, Tia complaining all the way.

Britt stood alone in the doorway, chin raised, back rigid, and so beautiful she made Jack ache. Something had gone wrong. A pang wrenched his heart, a pang he transformed into anger. "What is going on here?"

"I have a warrant, if you'd like to see it."

"I sure as hell would."

She pulled a document from her briefcase and extended it toward him in her long, graceful fingers. "Signed by Judge Banks this afternoon. I think you'll find it in order."

Blanking the sensual caress of those fingers from his mind, he gripped the paper, restraining himself from crumpling it in his fist. The warrant was in order all right. Nice and legal. He handed it back to her. "Now, what's *really* going on here?"

"The warrant explains everything you need to

know." She extended it toward him again. "Maybe you should read it more carefully."

"I doubt the warrant contains anything about what we shared this morning."

She didn't even flinch.

"What we shared doesn't matter anymore. *This afternoon* is business. *This morning* was a mistake."

Jack steeled himself against the painful throb claiming his neck and shoulders. She was wrong about this being business. His desire for the whole story was personal. Very personal. And the only way he could learn what was going on was to crack that cold, hard shell she'd erected between them. "So, do you sleep with defense attorneys as a matter of course, or did I garner special treatment?"

He felt like a rat the moment the words left his lips. And the raw stab of betrayal in her eyes made him feel even worse. She pursed her lips and said nothing. Instead of firing her to anger and inspiring her to blast him with her grievances, he'd only inflicted pain. "I didn't mean that, Britt. I'm sorry."

She tried to hide her vulnerability under a practiced glare. But try as she might, she couldn't erase the hurt etched in the fine lines around her eyes. "Sorry isn't going to cut it this time, Jack. I thought you were being honest with me. I had no idea you were still twisting the truth in some warped need to protect *the family*."

"Twisting the truth? How am I twisting the truth?"

"You're protecting a murderer, aren't you?"

Her argument was familiar. Ever since Tangi was killed, she'd believed Grant responsible. But she'd never accused *him* of protecting Grant with the same disgust she reserved for murderers, rapists, and other such scum. "Grant is no murderer. Besides, I'm his attorney. It's my job to protect him. You know damn well the system wouldn't work if we didn't both do our jobs."

"Save the defense attorney's rhetoric. You've taken your role a little too far."

What the hell was she talking about? Did she think he had invited her into his bed to take advantage of her? She couldn't think that, could she? "God, Britt, this morning—"

"I don't want to talk about this morn—" Her voice caught. She shook her head and refused to look at him, dismissing her emotion and him with a wave of her hand.

But she couldn't get rid of him that easily. He'd reached her. And this time he wouldn't let secrets get in the way. This time he'd plead his case. He'd throw himself on the mercy of the damned court if that's what it took. He'd lost Britt before. He'd move heaven and earth to keep from losing her again.

He skimmed her arm with his fingertips, the fabric of her suit as soft and warm as she'd been only a few short hours ago. "Whatever happened, we can fix it. It's worth it, Britt. This morning was no mirage."

Her chin quivered. She brushed the back of her hand across her eyes.

He cupped her elbow in his hand, afraid that if he exerted too much force the tenuous thread connecting them would break. "Come with me. We'll get out of this house. We'll talk. We'll get this straightened out."

Britt glanced over her shoulder at the bustle of activity in Grant's suite. Pain and mistrust waged war with questions in her eyes. For the moment, mistrust seemed to be winning.

Jack choked back a curse. She couldn't refuse to talk to him. He wouldn't let her. He had to know what was going on, why she had sneaked out of his place this afternoon, why she hadn't kept to their deal. He had to know where the questions in her eyes came from. "You can ask me anything, Britt. I'll tell you the truth."

She closed her eyes, long lashes brushing satin cheeks. "I'll give you five minutes, Jack. And I want the whole truth this time. No secrets." Opening her eyes, she spun and strode back into Grant's suite.

Jack waited in the doorway and watched the stiff determination in each step. He swallowed the anxiety pricking the back of his throat.

After a discussion with a pasty-faced detective, Britt returned to the spot where Jack waited. The chill of control in her eyes stabbed sharp and cold as an ice pick. She nodded. "Lead the way."

Britt followed him down the stairs and through the house to the sliding glass door opening to the patio. The house was quiet, no family member to be seen. The last thing he wanted was to run into Tia, or worse yet, Roger. He didn't need their input. He had to convince Britt he wasn't hiding anything from her. And judging from the mistrust in her eyes, it wouldn't be an easy task.

He slid open the door leading to the patio. Cold wind off the lake hit him full in the face. Bowing his head, he stepped outside, challenging the stiff blast.

Britt followed him, her head held high, her sharp eyes taking in the surroundings.

A wave of tenderness lapped at him. This woman

needed someone to take care of her. Someone to tell her she didn't always need to be brave. More than anything, he wanted that someone to be him. "Are you cold? We could go back in the house."

She shook her head, her eyes riveted on a spot beyond him.

He followed her gaze to the lakeshore.

Grant paced near the boathouse, his shoulders hunched, the collar of his coat flipped up to guard his face from the wind.

Damn. He'd forgotten Grant was patrolling the lakeshore, avoiding police and, most of all, family. "Let's go around front. My car—"

She broke away from his side and strode for the edge of the patio.

He hurried after her stiff back and flapping suit jacket, ready to grab her arm and drag her back inside the house should she get it in her head to confront Grant. But instead of making a beeline for Grant, she headed for the old stone chimney and the spot where they had talked last night.

Reaching the chimney, she stopped in its shelter and turned to face him. Though shadow cloaked her features, he recognized a question poised on her lips.

He drew close, his gut tightening, the blinding glare of the late afternoon sun in his eyes. "Go ahead and ask. What do you want to know?"

"Why did you hide evidence from the police?"

He almost laughed at the absurdity of her question. But one look at the serious set of her chin, and the chuckle caught in his throat. "Hide evidence? What the hell are you talking about?"

"You don't have to make up some story to cover your tracks, Jack. I tripped over the shoes myself."

"Shoes?" He realized his one-word echo sounded idiotic, but he had no idea what else to say.

Disappointment registered loud and clear in the downward tilt of her eyebrows and the grim line of her mouth. She paused for a moment as if to control her frustration. "Grant's shoes. Shoes covered in mud. Shoes that match the footprint left at the murder scene."

"You think I hid Grant's shoes?"

"I *know* you hid them. I found them myself. All I want to know is why. Why did you hide them? Why did you jeopardize your career, your ranch, your whole life to protect Grant? And why did you make love to me this morning?"

Her questions whirled through his confused mind like a child's spinning top, all detail a blur. "I don't know anything about muddy shoes, Britt. You'll have to enlighten me."

She exhaled a stream of pent-up frustration. Studying him a long moment, she seemed to penetrate his thoughts with her well-honed slivers of blue.

He stood straight, facing into the afternoon sun. From where she was standing she should be able to see every expression on his face, every emotion in his eyes. Good. He wanted her to read him, to witness his every thought and feeling. Maybe then she'd believe he didn't know what she was talking about. Maybe then she'd believe he wasn't hiding anything.

"Tell me what you found. Maybe we can figure this thing out together."

Britt leaned back against the chimney, the softness of her fair skin and wisps of pale gold hair contrasting with the rough-hewn stone. "Early this afternoon, I tripped over a bag in your study. The shoes spilled out of the bag." She pursed her lips, waiting for him to explain.

"And you think I hid the shoes to protect Grant?"

She nodded. "The store where Grant custom ordered them confirmed the purchase. They're his shoes. They were in your study. Are you telling me that you didn't know anything about them?"

He looked at her squarely. He had to make her believe him. "I don't know anything about muddy shoes in my study. I didn't touch them. I didn't touch the bag. I didn't know they were there."

As she studied him, the hard line of her brow seemed to soften. She sighed, the sound holding a note of clemency.

A spark of something kindled deep in his chest. Something warm, something bright, something like hope.

"If you didn't put the shoes in your study, how did they get there, Jack?"

He searched his memory but came up empty. "Hell if I know."

"No one stopped by for as much as a tea party? No one but you has access to your study?"

He shrugged. "Kimberly has a key. She and my mother take care of the place when I'm out of town."

Britt nodded, as if adding their names to her mental checklist.

"You don't think Kimberly or my mother—You're crazy."

"Am I, Jack? Would you rather I believe you're lying, and you hid the shoes yourself?"

He frowned and shook his head. "There has to be an explanation. What did the bag look like?"

"Tapestry. Some kind of tote bag."

Jack knew of only one person who carried a tapestry tote bag. A person who had every reason in the world to hide evidence implicating Grant. "Tia. Tia has a bag like that."

"Has she been in your study recently?"

Jack frowned. Tia had been in his study just yesterday, but try as he might, he couldn't remember her carrying her trademark tote bag.

He glanced over his shoulder toward the house. "I'll tell you everything I know about it, which isn't much. But first, I need to have a word with Tia."

She shook her head and raised her chin, glaring at him the way a prosecutor eyes a defendant when the guilty verdict is read. "It's a reflex with you, isn't it?"

She'd lost him. "A reflex?"

"Protecting people you care about. The family is threatened, and you cover up. You don't even realize you're doing it. It's ingrained. It's as natural for you as breathing."

Guilty as charged. He *did* protect people he cared about. He grew up protecting the family from Roger, and he'd expanded the mission in his chosen career. Sure, he protected those who needed it. He was proud of that fact. But the choice between protecting Tia and keeping his promise to Britt was an easy one. "Tia was in my study yesterday. But I don't remember her carrying her bag. I don't remember her carrying anything at all."

"Is there a chance Tia left the bag without you knowing? Maybe she was in your condo some other time."

He bit the inside of his lip. He wished he could tell her that Tia was to blame. He knew in his bones Tia was hiding something pertaining to Tangi's murder, but the more he thought about it the more certain he became that his sister-in-law had not had the tapestry bag with her when she stormed into his condo. "She was at my place once in the past week, and she wasn't carrying the bag. I'm sure of it."

Britt frowned, shaking her head in obvious frustration. "Are you telling me the whole truth? Please. I need you to be honest with me."

"I am being honest with you. You have to believe me. I'll never keep anything from you again."

Brow knitting, she stared at the ground between them. He could sense the war inside her. She wanted to believe him. Damn it, she *had* to believe him. He held his breath.

Finally, she met his eyes. "Give up the case, Jack. Let Grant hire another attorney. Let the family protect itself for a change."

He exhaled. Cold despair settled into his bones. "I can't do that. I can't walk away any more than you can. Grant isn't guilty. I can't let him be punished for something he didn't do."

She raised her chin, a tear glistening in the corner of one eye. "I have to do my thing, you have to do yours."

Jack nodded. She would have to rally the troops to convict Grant, and he would have to fight back with every weapon in his arsenal. "I love you, Britt. And you love me. Whatever happens, we'll get through this."

She swallowed hard and pursed her lips. "What if love isn't enough, Jack? It wasn't enough five years ago."

"Five years ago, I walked away *because* I loved you. I needed to protect you."

"I don't need protection, Jack. I never did."

He shook his head. "I'm not going anywhere, and neither are you. After this case is over, we'll work things out. Do you want to work things out?"

She didn't even blink. "More than anything."

He reached for her, pulling her softness against his chest, enfolding her in his arms.

A sound escaped her lips, a tender sigh from somewhere deep within her soul. Precious as a vow.

Jack soaked up the sound, locking it in his memory. "After this case is over, we'll work out everything. I can't lose you again. I won't—"

Looping her arms around his neck, she entwined her fingers in his hair and rested her head on his shoulder. Her breasts pressed against his chest. Her sweet breath fanned his throat. Everything about her felt so damned right.

A man cleared his throat behind them. "Counselor?"

Reluctantly, Jack stepped back and let his arms fall to his sides. After one last glance at Britt's flushed face and shining eyes, he turned in the direction of the voice. The skinny detective stepped toward them, his manner hesitant.

Britt brushed her eyes with the back of her hand and drew herself up. "What is it, Cassidy?"

"Baker found something. In the walk-in closet. You got to take a look."

Jack's stomach clenched.

Britt drew in a deep breath as if preparing to plunge over the first drop of a roller coaster. After a final glance at Jack, she followed Detective Cassidy toward the house.

Jack's stomach burned with the fire of a full-blown ulcer. What could the cop be referring to? Grant hadn't killed Tangi. Even now, Jack would stake his reputation on that fact. How could they find evidence in his bedroom? Unless...

Had Tia hidden the evidence? Had she hidden the shoes in his study?

Mulling over the questions in his mind, he followed the procession into the house and up the sweeping staircase. The cavernlike foyer was quiet. No whining, no complaining. The detective must have lived up to his promise of shepherding Tia out of the way. Hopefully she hadn't gone far. If he found out she had hidden the shoes and whatever was in the closet, he'd gift-wrap her and hand her over to Britt himself.

He hadn't been in the suite since Tia's remodeling binge, and the opulence made him cringe. Silk and velvet covered everything from the walls to the four-poster king-sized bed, and in such an array of colors, it made his head whirl. The place looked like either the lair of medieval royalty or a high-class bordello. Tia never ceased to amaze him.

Jack turned away from the appalling room and followed Britt and the detective into a clothing-crammed closet bigger than most people's living rooms. Detective Cassidy knelt next to a shoe rack. Under the neatly stored shoes curled a man's starched white shirt. Even from a distance, Jack could see the brown stains on the shirt's sleeves were probably dried blood. Near one sleeve, looking as if they'd tumbled out of the pocket, two diamond earrings glittered in

the overhead light. Their settings arched into letters—
TR. Tangi Rowe.

His stomach seized.

Britt turned to the detective. "This is plenty for an
arrest. Go ahead."

Jack said nothing. He couldn't. Not with the blood
evidence staring him in the face. Not with Britt standing so close, anguish shining from her eyes.

The detective brushed past Jack on his way downstairs.

BRITT FOLLOWED Cassidy out the kitchen door and
across the patio.

Jack walked close behind across the leaf-strewn
grass. So close she could almost smell his scent over
the cold breeze off the lake, almost feel his heat and
the hard planes of his body.

Here she was, about to start the process which
would bring Tangi's murderer to justice, and all she
could think about was the man behind her, the warmth
of his embrace, the passion in his promise. She
wanted to believe him. With every fiber of her being,
she wanted to love him.

She forced herself to focus on the silhouette pacing
the shoreline. Head down and shoulders slumped,
Grant looked like he'd just suffered one hell of a beating.

Britt stretched her stride, catching up with Cassidy's choppy gait. Thoughts of the pain Tangi must
have suffered before she died stabbed through any
trace of pity she might have felt for Jack's brother.
He deserved what he got. And more. He deserved to
rot in hell.

And she'd arrange it for him. She wouldn't allow

the feelings Jack touched deep inside her to deter her. Until this trial was over, Jack was nothing more than another defense attorney protecting his client.

And maybe if she chanted this thought to herself enough, she could get through the next months without rushing into his arms.

Bearing down on Grant, Cassidy reached for his handcuffs, fumbling them from his belt. The cuffs hit the ground with a metallic clatter, and the party came to a halt. Cassidy stooped to pick them up off the grass.

Britt tried not to roll her eyes in disgust. Since the morning the county sheriff's department had discovered Tangi's body, Britt had pictured calm, efficient Al Mylinski officiating at this moment. Truth was, she'd prefer anyone to the bumbling Dan Cassidy. Good thing she was here to make sure Cassidy didn't forget to read Grant his rights. With Jack watching every move, this arrest had to be textbook. And she would make sure it was, down to the letter. Grant would not be set free due to one of Cassidy's trademark mistakes.

Cassidy cleared his throat with a horrible grating growl.

Grant turned toward them, his face waxen, his eyes dead. "You're here to arrest me."

Britt nodded.

Grant looked past her to Jack.

"Don't say anything, Grant. Not one more word. Trust me."

Trust me. Jack's words spiraled through Britt's mind like a flipping coin. She met his dark gaze and held it for a long moment. Finally, she nodded to Cassidy.

The detective grabbed Grant's arms and pulled them behind his back. He clasped the handcuffs first around one wrist, then the other. Metal clicked against metal, locking tight. "Grant Alcott, you are under arrest for the murder of Tangi Rowe. You have the right to remain silent..."

Chapter Twelve

Britt slumped behind the wheel of her car. Thank God for Al Mylinski. He would oversee the rest of the search. She could get away from the Alcott mansion—away from Jack—and think.

In the few minutes she'd been alone with him, he'd jumbled her thoughts and feelings so badly she had no clear idea of where logic ended and emotion began. She ached to curl up in his arms and forget the truth, forget her job, forget everything that made her who she was. Being around him even one moment longer would only confuse her more.

Fingers trembling, she twisted the key in the ignition, the engine sparking to life. She jammed the car into gear and headed down the cobblestone drive in the direction Cassidy had taken Grant. The City County building was a couple of miles away. She'd be safely ensconced in her office in minutes.

Turning out of the Alcott driveway and onto the quiet street, she glanced in the rear view mirror just in time to spot Jack ducking into his Jaguar.

Her pulse thrummed in her neck. She couldn't handle seeing him again. Not now. Not this soon. She needed to get some distance first. Gain some perspective. She needed to bury her emotions in evidence and the cold, hard truth. Then she could face him. She could pour herself into Grant's trial until she and Jack were in a position to work through their problems and be together.

She accelerated on twisting Farwell Drive, a black sedan falling in behind her, putting distance between her car and Jack's Jaguar.

A black sedan.

Visions of a black sedan racing toward her in the parking ramp flashed through her mind. She looked into the rearview mirror again. Couldn't be. No killer in his right mind would follow her so closely on a quiet lakeside road in broad daylight.

Jack had her so shaken she was imagining things. Gulping in a few deep breaths, she tuned the car radio to the classical station and glanced in the rearview mirror once again.

The black car behind her followed close. Too close. She eased her foot off the accelerator, giving the obnoxious driver ample opportunity to pass. Jack was somewhere behind that car, and although she couldn't talk to him right now, she longed for the comfort of seeing his face in the rearview mirror.

She took the next bend slower, the thick stands of maple, oak, and birch on either side of the road masking the imposing lake homes and her view of the curve ahead.

The black car pulled up close behind her, its bumper nearly hanging on hers.

Then she felt the thump.

Her head snapped back. "What the—" She struggled to regain control of her car.

The sedan slammed her again.

Her tires screeched. She spun the wheel, narrowly missing a maple.

The car hit again.

Metal crunched. Tires squealed. A tree trunk filled Britt's vision. She gripped the wheel, straining to turn. A scream of tangled steel pierced her ears. Her head snapped forward.

Then silence.

JACK SCREECHED his car to a stop, his heart pounding in his ears. He'd witnessed the crash, every excruciating moment of it, and now one thought jangled through his mind. *Britt has to be all right. She just has to be.*

He threw open the Jag's door and dashed to her car. The afternoon sun glared off the gnarled steel of the hood, its front end smashed against a huge maple like a folded accordion. Cracks spider-webbed the windshield, glinting in the setting sun.

As his brain registered every detail, his hands seemed to move of their own accord, grabbing the handle of the driver's door, forcing the bent metal open. His pulse thundered in his ears, drowning out the metallic groan of the battered door, the clap of waves against rock, the cries of Canadian geese in the sky overhead.

Britt lay still, her head resting against the back of her seat, an angry red mark already visible on her forehead. Her seat belt stretched across her chest, pinning her to the seat. She gasped for a deep breath, her eyelids fluttering.

A crashing wave of relief almost knocked Jack to the ground. She was alive. Thank God she was alive.

He crouched beside her and ran his fingers over her cool cheek. "Britt?"

She moved her head and groaned.

The sound of her pain sliced Jack to the core. He had to do something. He had to get help. He sprang to his feet and glanced around. The black car rested on the opposite side of the street, entangled in a clump of white-barked birch trees. Past the birches, the roof of a large brick Tudor home jutted against the glare of the setting sun. A man perched atop a ladder outside a third-story window stared in his direction, a squeegee poised in his fist.

Jack cupped his hands around his mouth and called to the man. "Call 911. We need an ambulance and the police."

The man saluted with the squeegee and descended the ladder.

Jack crouched next to Britt. Her cheek felt colder, the red mark on her forehead transforming into a welt. "Britt? Please hear me."

She stirred again. This time her eyes opened and focused on his face. "Jack?"

"You were in a car accident."

Her eyes looked dark, haunted. She raised her head, her face puckering into a grimace of pain.

"Take it easy. You might have a concussion. An ambulance is on the way."

She grabbed the wheel, pulling herself upright as if she planned to climb from the seat. "The other car. The driver ran me off the road. He tried to kill me."

Jack guided her back against the seat. "I know. I saw everything. An ambulance and the police should be here any minute. Now lie still. I'll be right back."

Britt rested her head against the seat. Her breath rose from her lips in a steamy cloud.

The scent of a wood fire carried on the frosty wind, a reminder of distant warmth. He shrugged out of his coat and draped it over Britt.

Where was that ambulance? Where were the police? He checked his watch. Only a minute had passed since he'd called to the window washer, a minute that crept like an hour. With one last glance at her pale face and glazed eyes, he headed across the street. His heartbeat accelerated with each step. The driver had tried to kill Britt three times now. Jack would make sure he didn't get another chance. If the driver hadn't died in the crash, Jack would make him wish he had.

The black car rested in the Tudor's massive front grounds. Slender white birch trunks jutted around the sedan's dark shape like spears, some triumphant, some broken in battle. Dodging a roadside bed of frost-shriveled geraniums, he approached the car and peered in the driver's window.

Tia sat trapped between the seat and a slowly deflating air bag. Face flushed, she stared at him with glassy dark eyes.

Tia. Rage inflamed his bloodstream like a shot of whiskey. He closed the distance to the car in three strides. Reaching around a tree trunk, he wrenched open the door as wide as the birches would allow. Unfortunately, the space wasn't wide enough for him to strangle his sister-in-law. "What the hell are you up to, Tia? Have you lost your mind?"

At the force of his bellow, she shrank away from the opening. The sweet stench of alcohol wafted from the car. Red speckled her face, the windows, and the air bag. Wine, not blood.

Jack clenched his fists. He needed answers, and by God, Tia was going to provide them. "Tia, I'm going to ask you a question and if you value your life, you'll answer. Why are you trying to kill Britt?"

She narrowed her dark eyes, focusing over Jack's shoulder. An expression of rabid hatred twisted her face. "Get her away from me, Jack. Get her the hell away."

Britt's sharp intake of breath whispered in his ear. He spun to face her.

Face pale, she leaned against the sedan for support. "Tia? You're the one trying to kill me? Why?"

He grasped her arm to steady her. "Britt, you need to sit down."

She tried to shrug off his grip, the intensity of her voice rising. "You sabotaged the furnace in my house? You almost killed my father!"

"What did you expect me to do? Just sit by and let *you* send Grant to prison?"

Jack's muscles tensed. Leave it to Tia to make things worse. Now that she'd all but admitted to protecting Grant, he'd never convince Britt to sit quietly and wait for the ambulance. "Shut up, Tia. You need a lawyer."

"But you're my lawyer, aren't you?"

"Not anymore. I'm Grant's lawyer. And as of this moment, your interests conflict with Grant's."

Conflict of interest aside, he couldn't represent Tia. Not when he'd just as soon strangle her as look at her. His loyalty in *this* matter belonged to Britt. Every shred of it. "This is the last advice I'm giving you, Tia. From now on, you're on your own."

Tia tossed her black hair and glared out of the sliver of an opening. "Your advice is worth about as much as your loyalty. Just wait until I tell Roger how you sold out the family for *her*."

Jack gritted his teeth.

"Tell Roger anything you like." He stepped closer to Britt, trying to guide her away from the black car.

Despite his grip on her arm, she shifted closer to the open door. "I know how much you wanted a baby, Tia. It must have killed you to learn another woman was pregnant with Grant's child."

Tia's glare darted to Britt, color deepening in her cheeks.

Ever the D.A. and intuitive to boot. A few more jabs like that and Tia would explode, incriminating herself in a fit of self-righteous rage. He'd warned Tia to keep her mouth shut. If she wanted to ignore his advice and incriminate herself, she had the right. But there was something more important at stake. Namely, Britt's health. "There'll be time for questions later. Now you have to sit down before you fall down."

Britt wrenched her arm free from his grasp, wobbling with the effort. "Grant lied to you about the blackmail. He *wanted* to give Tangi the money. He loved Tangi."

Pure hatred twisted Tia's scarlet lips into a snarl.

"Tia, what else has Grant lied to you about? Why are you protecting him?"

A siren split the charged air. The ambulance and police had arrived. And none too soon. Jack grasped Britt's shoulders. Her whole body shook with the exertion of standing. "That's enough, Britt. The police will take it from here."

She fought off his grip, straining to see around him.

"Grant was having a child with Tangi, not with you, Tia. How did that make you feel?"

A police car pulled behind Britt's wrecked Corsica and stopped. Two uniformed officers stepped out.

Still holding Britt's shoulders, Jack motioned to the cops with his head.

Britt spotted the officers too. She lunged toward Tia with renewed vigor. "Were you afraid Grant would divorce you and leave you with nothing, Tia? Did *you* kill Tangi?"

"I didn't kill her. And if you think I'm sorry *he* did, you're out of your mind."

Jack's blood froze. Damn Tia. Damn her and her false alibi. She wasn't protecting Grant, she was burying him. She was throwing shovelful after shovelful of dirt on his body and Jack couldn't do a damn thing to stop it.

Britt stepped to the side where she had an unobstructed view of Tia. "What are you saying? That Grant killed Tangi?"

Tia's voice rose in disbelief. "You're the one that had him arrested."

Britt cocked her head. "But Tia, you told the police he was with you the night Tangi was killed. Are you now saying he *wasn't* with you?"

A whimper slipped from Tia's lips. Apparently she'd realized what she'd said. Too late.

Britt met Jack's eyes. The look lasted but a moment, long enough for him to read the triumph in their blue depths loud and clear.

A leaden weight descended on his shoulders.

"Tia, did you hide your tapestry bag in Jack's condo? The tapestry bag containing shoes Grant wore the night he killed Tangi?"

"My bag? Did I— No. I don't know what happened to that bag." Tia glared at Jack, her eyes hot and accusing, as if she blamed him for her outburst. "If Grant's shoes were in Jack's condo, maybe *he* put them there. Maybe he's covering for Grant, just like me. Just like the family has always covered for Grant."

Jack let his hands drop limp by his sides, heavy, useless. It wasn't enough for Tia to bury herself and Grant, she had to drag him along too. He studied the frozen geraniums under his feet.

Britt's hot gaze moved over his face. "Tia, the next time you're questioned about Grant's muddy shoes, you might want to try answering with the truth. Jack already told me he didn't hide them. And I believe him."

Jack looked into her eyes. Relief seeped into him like the heat of a fire on a cold dark night. The trust he saw there told him everything he needed to know.

"DAD, WE HAVE TO TALK." Britt bent to kiss her father's cheek. She'd spent a long sleepless night in the hospital, the nurses waking her every half hour to check her vital signs. Then her doctor had ordered tests that wasted most of the day. When the doctor said he was keeping her overnight for observation, he wasn't kidding. She felt thoroughly observed.

Before she headed home for some real sleep and to try to patch her life together, she had to face her father. She had to hear from his own lips the reason he'd accepted bribes from Roger Alcott.

She reached for the privacy curtain and pulled it around her dad's bed. Now that he'd been taken off the respirator, he'd been moved into a normal room, quiet compared to the bustle of Intensive Care. Good thing. She didn't need an army of doctors and nurses overhearing their conversation.

She moved several potted plants and sat on the windowsill, the setting sun's scalding rays doing nothing to dispel the chill in her bones.

Her dad pressed a button, adjusting his bed to a sitting position. "What is it, hon?"

Her mouth grew dry, gritty, as if it was filled with sand. He'd been through so much. And now she, his own daughter, was about to accuse him of accepting bribes. How had things come to this? "I talked to Jack a couple days ago."

His expression didn't change, but the lines surrounding his pale lips deepened to creases, and dark circles sagged under his eyes.

Britt shifted on the hard windowsill. "Jack thinks you accepted bribes from Rico Gianni."

Her dad's skin took on a gray cast, as if the shadow of a ghost passed over him. He shifted his eyes to stare at the blank screen of the television over his bed.

"Is it true?"

He swallowed. His mouth moved but no sound came out.

He clutched the white sheet in one fist.

Nurses' voices filtered through the curtain. The minute hand of the clock opposite his bed clicked ahead one minute. Two minutes.

The sun burned into Britt's back. His silence burned into her soul. "Did Gianni pay you to sabotage cases against him and his associates? Did one of those associates hire Jimmy Surles to shoot you when you tried to back out?"

He flinched as if she'd slapped him across the face.

Tears filled his eyes and ran down his cheeks in little rivers.

The clock's hand clicked off another minute.

He swallowed his tears and cleared his throat. "I could never afford to give you and your mother everything you deserved."

The anguish in his words pierced her heart.

"You gave us everything, Dad. You were a great husband to Mom, and I can't imagine having a better father."

He held up a hand. "You've always wanted to believe the people you loved were perfect. Ever since you were a little girl. Your mother and I—I think we would have given almost anything to live up to the faith you placed in us. I would still give anything."

Britt's heart seemed to stutter. "You've always been the perfect father to me."

"Please. How can you say that now that you know the truth?"

"Tell me the whole truth, Dad. That's what I'm asking for."

He nodded slowly. Sadly.

A calmness worked up her spine and spread over her. A numbness. She clenched her hands into fists, preparing herself for the story to come.

"Many years ago, before you started law school, I made a deal with the devil." He paused, his face twisting with regret. "Rico Gianni paid me and another detective to look the other way during our investigation of a truck hijacking. And that was only the beginning."

Britt nodded. Even though she'd already heard the facts from Jack, her dad's words still stole her breath away. She focused on the clock and waited for his words to sink in, waited for the numbness to clear from her head.

"After that, he called on me to fix things for him and his friends or to feed him information. Every time I tried to back away, he'd threaten to tell what I'd done. He swore he'd ruin my career. My family." He gulped air. "I thought it would be over when he went away on that racketeering charge, but then his friends got involved. Apparently it became public knowledge. I knew I was in trouble when Roger Alcott got into the act."

Britt's heart stuttered. "Roger bribed you, too?"

"No. He just wanted me to discourage you from marrying Jack. He said the daughter of a dirty cop wasn't good enough to marry an Alcott. The bastard."

She cleared her throat. There was one thing she needed to know. One question she had to ask. "Dad, why did you take Gianni's money in the first place?" She held her breath. He would explain. He had to.

He stared at the white sheets clenched in his fist. "Because I wanted the money, Britt. Because I was weak and I wanted the money."

She leaned back against the hot window glass. Her life, her illusions, had crumbled to dust, and all she could do was sit and listen to the hands of the clock. She'd insisted on the cold hard truth, and she'd gotten it. Now she had to figure out a way to deal with it. "I have to go, Dad. I need some time to think."

He met her gaze, his cheeks wet with tears. "I prayed you'd never find out, Britt. I prayed you'd never know. The thing I feared most was the look in your eyes. The dead, cynical look. The look you have right now."

Her stomach wrenched. She was going to be sick. Or faint. She jumped to her feet. Clawing the privacy curtain aside, she ran from the room. Ran from her dad's quiet words. Ran from the truth.

"OF COURSE, I love my dad as much as I always have. But now that he's home, it's hard to look into his eyes." Tearing her gaze from the warmth of Jack's face, Britt looked down at her blueberry bagel and coffee with distaste. Since the day two weeks ago when she'd forced the truth from her father, she'd struggled with more than her appetite. The sting of betrayal still pierced her heart like a sharp and deadly blade.

The strain of facing Jack during Grant's preliminary hearing hadn't helped. Sitting across from him in the courtroom hour after hour without sharing his thoughts, his touch, his comforting warmth was almost too much. Giving up on the bagel, she met his eyes once again, soaking up the solace she found nowhere else.

He reached across the scarred table of the Easy Street Cafe and enfolded her hand in his. "Give it some time, Britt. It takes time to forgive someone."

"It's not me I'm worried about. It's him. He never sleeps, he hardly ever talks, and his eyes are filled with such self-loathing it scares me. Anything I say seems to make things worse."

Jack moved his fingers over her hand and wrist, stroking, caressing, soothing. "It takes even longer to forgive yourself."

From the burning intensity in his eyes, Britt could tell he was talking not only of her father, but of himself. She squeezed his hand. "It was so hard to get through the hearing without walking over and touching you. I thought it would drive me crazy.''

A mischievous grin crooked a corner of his lips. ''I would have liked to see the expression on Judge Banks' face if you had.''

Britt returned the smile and raised an eyebrow. ''Disorder in the court?''

''I wouldn't have objected.''

She drew in a deep breath. After the turmoil she'd endured over the last months and the maelstrom she was about to face with the commencement of Grant's trial, this little reprieve was like a wisp of fresh country air. The chance to touch Jack's hand, to share his laughter, and to speak her heart was a precious, if short, recess. ''It's going to be a long trial. I'll miss talking to you and joking around like this. With the strain between my dad and me, I have no one else.''

The smile dropped from his lips and he looked deep into her eyes as if he was searching her soul. ''We're worth it, you know, the waiting.''

She entwined her fingers in his, savoring every second of his touch. ''I know.''

''And we each have to give this trial our all. Anything less wouldn't be honest.''

He was right. One of the things she loved in him was his commitment to what he felt was right. And she had an equally strong commitment. To allow their relationship to interfere in this case would be a betrayal for them both. ''I know. We'll get through this.''

He released her hand and reached under the table for his briefcase. After flipping open the latches, he withdrew a thick document and laid it on the table in front of her. ''Just remember, Britt, I love you.''

Tingles stole up her spine at his soft words. She held his gaze for a long time, not wanting to sever the contact. When she knew she was ready, she looked down at the sheaf of paper.

"It's my motion to suppress the muddy shoes. The hearing is scheduled for Friday afternoon in Judge Banks' chambers."

She nodded and set her chin. Not only would she get through this trial, she'd give it everything she had to give. And she had no doubt that Jack would too. She had to keep her promise to Tangi, and he had to do his best to protect his brother. They had to be true to themselves. In this, they could not compromise.

Chapter Thirteen

"Glad you could make it, Ms. Gerritsen." Judge Banks sat back in his chair, crossing his arms over his chest, his belly bulging in front of him like a paunchy Buddha after a full meal. He pointed to his watch. "The clock is ticking."

Britt flinched inwardly and closed the door to the judge's chambers behind her. "Sorry I'm late, Your Honor."

Without glancing at Jack and Kyle Ayres already seated in front of the judge's massive desk, Britt found her way to a chair. Her biceps ached with the weight of half a dozen file folders, heavy as stone tablets. She piled them and her briefcase on the floor, picked the top folder off the stack, and spread it open in her lap.

She withdrew the thick legal document from the file folder. Since Jack had given her his motion, she'd sacrificed sleep to research case law and prepare the people's response. She was as ready as she'd ever be. Jack would *not* convince the judge to rule the muddy shoes inadmissible in Grant's trial. Not if she had anything to say about it.

Smoothing his tie, Judge Banks glanced down at

his desk clock and frowned. "Let's get this underway. Don't make me regret staying late on my afternoon off. I have a four o'clock tee-off time at University Ridge, and I'm going to be very cranky if I miss my last golf outing before winter."

Jack smiled, sympathy for the judge's plight written all over his face. "This shouldn't take long, Your Honor. My argument is very simple."

Britt fingered the motion to suppress. Simple? Right. So simple it took a document the length of a short novel to explain.

She offered the judge a smile of her own. Instead of sympathetic, the smile felt wooden, achingly false. Apparently one had to grow up in country clubs to appreciate the gravity of a missed golf outing. No matter. She'd confronted the brotherhood of golf plenty of times and won. This time would be no different.

She glanced at her watch to cover for her lack of commiseration. "Four o'clock shouldn't be a problem, Your Honor. My position is also simple."

"With all these simple positions, it's a wonder we have to hold this hearing at all," Judge Banks said, sarcasm oozing from his voice. He nodded to the court reporter seated to his left.

The young woman positioned her fingers over the keys, ready to etch every word vocalized into the permanent court record.

The judge swung his gaze back to Jack. "Let's hear that simple argument, Mr. Alcott. Short and sweet."

Jack glanced in Britt's direction and for a moment, their eyes met. He offered her a small smile.

A delicious tremor shook Britt to her toes. Under the open file folder, she dug her fingernails into her palms. "Go ahead, Counselor. I can't wait to hear what you've come up with."

Jack turned back to the judge with the self-satisfied calm of a poker player holding all the cards. "This is a clear-cut illegal search, Your Honor. A blatant violation of my client's Fourth Amendment rights. As an assistant district attorney, Ms. Gerritsen is an agent of the government. She can't conduct a search of my study without a warrant. The shoes she found as a result of that illegal search should be deemed inadmissible."

Judge Banks turned his impatient glower on Britt. "And Ms. Gerritsen, how do you plan to convince the court that your search was legal?"

Britt drew in a deep breath and summoned a confident smile to her lips. "There are three points Mr. Alcott has left out of his little spiel, Your Honor. First, he invited me into his house. Secondly, I was there not as an agent of the government, but as a private citizen. And thirdly, I did not conduct a search of the premises. I tripped over the tapestry bag, and the shoes in question spilled out onto the floor. The bag was in plain sight."

Jack scoffed and shook his head as if she'd just said the most ridiculous lie he'd ever heard. "I invited her to enter my condominium, Your Honor, not to search it. And I never extended that invitation to include my study. I do not do social entertaining in my study. She had no business in there. Besides, she can't act as an agent of the government one minute and then a private citizen when it suits her."

"Your Honor, Mr. Alcott is twisting—"

Judge Banks held up a hand to silence her. His glower turned to full-fledged scowl. "There's a good reason we try to prevent personal relationships from mingling with the law. This sounds more like a lovers' spat than a hearing. Ms. Gerritsen, is it true that Neil Fitzroy plans to argue this case himself?''

Jack's head snapped around.

Britt's mouth went dry. Judge Banks had heard the latest rumor. She *wished* it was a rumor. It was the truth. And now Jack knew it too. And judging from his beaming smile, he wasn't too upset about the news. With her off the case, the door would be wide open for them to pick up their relationship. He was probably already planning weekend getaways and late-night rendezvous. Maybe she should be happy, too. But the thought of someone else trying Tangi's case didn't sit right. Even if the someone was the District Attorney himself.

''Well? Is Fitzroy planning to take over the case, Ms. Gerritsen?''

She shoved away her thoughts of the future and focused on the question at hand. ''I haven't been officially notified, Your Honor.''

The judge shook his head and glanced at his watch. ''Fitz is a politician to the end. He's probably waiting to see how I rule on his evidence. Very well, let's proceed, but I'd like to hear more law and less he said, she said. And I'd like to hear it quick.''

Kyle handed Jack a thick file folder. Jack flipped open the cover, but didn't even glance at the contents. ''Your Honor, in the case of the state of Arizona versus Stephen Taylor, the court ruled—''

''I've read your motion, Mr. Alcott. I'm aware of the case law you use to support your argument.''

Jack held up a hand. ''One moment, Your Honor. I'd like to point out to the court that since the discovery of the shoes was the probable cause used to obtain the search warrant, everything the prosecution found in my client's bedroom should be considered inadmissible as well. The illegal search taints the prosecution's entire case. It's all fruit of the poisonous tree."

Britt cringed. Just as she'd feared, the whole case against Grant rested on the outcome of this hearing. And she'd better not blow it.

Judge Banks nodded. "Your argument is noted, Mr. Alcott. I'll take that into account *after* I rule on the shoes. Right now, I'm more curious about how Ms. Gerritsen plans to justify her actions."

Pressure throbbed behind Britt's eyes. She had to word her argument carefully if she was to dig herself out of this hole.

The heat of Jack's gaze skimmed over her. She didn't dare return his stare. One look, and she'd be undone. She had to keep her mind on the law. The evidence, the law, and the truth were the only things that mattered now.

A loud knock sounded on the door.

Judge Banks raised his bushy eyebrows. "Enter."

Britt, Jack, and Kyle craned their necks toward the door.

Mahogany swung wide, and Al Mylinski strode into the judge's chambers. "Your Honor, sorry for the intrusion, but I have to talk to Ms. Gerritsen. It's urgent."

Britt's heart flip-flopped in her chest. She jumped to her feet, upsetting the stack of manila file folders. Paper strewed across the floor.

Judge Banks glared at her, the excess skin under his chin making him look like an annoyed snapping turtle. "I don't appreciate this, Ms. Gerritsen. But I'll give you two minutes to talk to your detective. Not a second more."

"Thank you, Your Honor. I'll make it quick."

"You'd better."

Leaving the scattered papers, Britt scurried out of the judge's chambers after Mylinski. Once out in the hall, she drew in a deep breath, trying to calm her jangling nerves.

His forehead furrowed with concern and his eyes held more than a hint of regret. "Sorry about that, but I've got to talk to you."

Britt squinted into Mylinski's flushed face. He wouldn't have interrupted the hearing if his news wasn't important. And from his expression, she would be trudging, not dancing, back into the judge's chambers once she heard it. "It must be bad news."

He nodded, mouth set in a grim line.

Great. Another problem. The last thing she needed this afternoon. "Go ahead. I'm getting used to bad news."

"I got a report from the lab. A fingerprint report."

"Were they able to lift prints from the bloody shirt we found?" She knew lifting prints from the rough fabric or tiny buttons of a dress shirt was a long shot, but only something this big would cause Mylinski to invade Judge Banks' chambers in the middle of a hearing.

"I asked them to take a look at the tapestry bag. They lifted two good prints from the handle."

Cold foreboding slithered over Britt's skin. Someone's prints other than Grant's and Tia's would give Jack an alternate murderer to present to the jury. That is, if Britt could get the evidence admitted to court in the first place. "Whose prints are they? Do they muddy our case?"

"One print belongs to Tia Alcott."

Britt relaxed ever so slightly. "No surprise there. It's her bag. And we're surmising she hid the bag to protect Grant."

Mylinski stiffened.

An ominous shiver clambered up the length of her spine. She drew in a deep breath. "Who does the other print belong to?"

Mylinski focused on a spot somewhere over her head. "Jack Alcott."

Britt froze, ice reaching into her veins. Ice, and then fire. It couldn't be. It just couldn't be. Jack had sworn he didn't know anything about the bag. Or the shoes. He'd promised to tell her the truth. He'd promised he would never keep anything from her again. He couldn't have lied to her. "It could be an old print. He could have touched the bag months ago."

Mylinski shook his head, his movement slow and inevitable as doom. "Unlikely. You saw Tia carrying that bag. Other witnesses saw Tia carrying that bag. If Jack had touched it more than a few days before you found it, his prints would have been smudged past the point of recognition. I know you don't want to hear this, Britt, but Jack Alcott touched that bag sometime *after* Tangi Rowe's death."

Britt shook her head hard, as if doing so would shuffle Mylinski's words into something that made sense. "He said he didn't know how the bag got into his condo. He wouldn't lie to me."

"The evidence speaks for itself, Britt."

The evidence. Cold, impartial evidence. Her protests died in her throat. Nausea lapped at her self-control. She had trusted Jack. *Trusted him.* And he had lied to her. He had looked her straight in the eye, promised to always tell her the truth, and then he had *lied.* Heat tore through her body, numbness stuttered through her mind, and agony screamed in her heart.

"You've got to consider charging Jack with obstruction, Britt."

Jack? Charged with obstruction of justice? Even with the scorching torment of Jack's betrayal racing through her veins, she couldn't believe what Mylinski was suggesting. "Don't be ridiculous, Al."

Mylinski fumbled in his pockets, coming up empty. Finally he leveled his gaze on her, his eyes clouding with dismay. "I hoped you could be impartial about this case. But you're letting your personal relationship with Jack Alcott influence you."

His words stabbed deep and hit bone. She'd promised herself she wouldn't let her love for Jack botch up Tangi's case. She'd promised herself she'd let the evidence guide her. The evidence, the law, and the truth. "Oh God, what do I do?"

After checking his pockets one more time, Mylinski let his hands hang limp by his sides. "You got two choices. You charge him or you don't. You charge him and you get him disbarred, you ruin his career, the money supply dries up for those kids at his ranch. Not to mention that he never forgives you. And for what? The judge might throw out our evidence. Tangi's murderer goes free, and Jack gets disbarred anyway."

She'd hashed out the possible repercussions in her mind the afternoon she'd tripped over the tapestry bag in Jack's study. Hearing the words from Al was enough to make her break into a cold sweat.

Mylinski shrugged. "And if you don't charge him, nothing happens."

"Except that he gets away with breaking the law."

"Right."

Nausea crashed over her like waves colliding with the shore. Family or not, how could Jack risk everything he'd worked for to protect a murderer? How could he lie to her, betray her? Raising her chin, she smoothed her clammy palms over her wool skirt. "This is my call, Al. When the time comes, I'll make it."

Mylinski gave her a single nod and stepped to the side.

Ignoring the rolling of her stomach, she trudged past Mylinski and into Judge Banks' chambers.

All eyes focused on her as she stooped and gathered up her spilled file. The paper rattled in her shaking fingers, her distress audible in the charged stillness of the judge's chambers.

Collecting the last of her papers, she took her place in her chair. Though she felt Jack's gaze on her, she couldn't bear even one glance in his direction. Questions swirled in her mind. How could he have betrayed her? How could he have lied to her? And what was she going to do about it? She'd told Mylinski it was her decision to make, and she'd make it. But at the moment, she didn't have the first clue what her decision would be.

Judge Banks placed his beefy elbows on his desk, his chair creaking under his shifting weight. "I trust you straightened everything out with your detective, Ms. Gerritsen?"

She sat stiff as a military prosecutor at a court martial, her back aching with the effort, her heart aching with each beat. "Your Honor, some new evidence has been brought to my attention. Evidence that may have a bearing on your decision."

"Well, don't keep us in suspense, Counselor. Let's hear it."

Britt forced herself to ignore the hot pressure of Jack's gaze, the answering pressure in her chest. She focused on the mahogany bookshelves lining the chamber walls, each shelf laden with thick leather-bound law books. The shelves seemed to sway, to close in on her. The gold lettering on each volume glinted in the afternoon sun streaming through the windows.

She swallowed her anguish, infusing her voice with what strength she could muster. "Jackson Alcott's fingerprints have been recovered from the handle of the bag used to conceal the muddy shoes. It's the people's contention that Mr. Alcott was concealing the evidence in question to protect his client."

Jack shot up out of his chair. "What the hell?"

"Sit down, Counselor," the judge barked.

Jack stepped toward her. "You don't believe—"

She swallowed hard and looked into his eyes. Eyes she had made the mistake of trusting. Of loving. "I believe the evidence, Jack. It's the only thing I *can* believe."

"I see." A calmness suffused Jack's face as if he had willed the lines in his forehead, the creases around his mouth to disappear. He lowered himself back into his chair, his face expressionless as a master poker player's. "Your Honor, there was no such concealment in this case, and Ms. Gerritsen knows it. If she truly thought I concealed the bag, she should have charged me with obstruction of justice. She has made no such charge. Nor will she.''

Damn Jack. He thought she was bluffing and he was calling her hand. He didn't believe she had the guts, the conviction to charge him with his crime.

Or maybe he was banking on her love for him. Maybe he believed that for him, she'd overlook the law.

Judge Banks cocked an eyebrow in her direction. ''Ms. Gerritsen?''

All eyes drilled into her. Judge Banks', the court reporter's, Kyle Ayres', and Jack's.

Jack. Britt could still hear the tenderness in his voice after the sedan had almost run her down in the parking garage. She could see his concern as he slumped in the hospital corridor waiting for her, the first sparks of dawn glinting off that lock of hair drooped onto his forehead. She could taste the life-giving warmth of his kiss after he'd told her the truth about her father. And feel his passion when they'd made love.

A lead weight descended on her chest. She couldn't breathe. Couldn't think. She could only feel. God help her, she loved Jack Alcott. She loved him with all her heart.

But love wasn't enough.

She stood on shaky legs and walked to the door of the judge's chamber. Grasping the cold knob, she pulled it open.

Mylinski stood outside, as if he knew she'd be calling for him.

And of course, he did. He knew it all along. There was only one choice she could make. ''Detective? Will you come in here, please?''

Mylinski shuffled inside.

Jack stared at her. ''Britt.''

She dragged in a deep breath. She couldn't look at him. The last thing she wanted was to see the deception, the betrayal in his dark eyes. The moment he'd uttered his lie, he'd severed the precious, delicate thread that connected them. He'd destroyed her trust and her heart. And now he had destroyed himself. She concentrated on the floor, on the law books, on the judge's belly, on Kyle's glasses, on anything, anyone but Jack.

''Britt. I told you the truth. You have to believe me.''

Her throat seized. No matter how much she wanted to, she couldn't believe him. And for that, she'd never forgive him. ''Detective, I want you to arrest Mr. Alcott. The charges are obstruction of justice and accessory after the fact.''

Chapter Fourteen

Britt stumbled from the judge's chambers, her legs so shaky she could barely balance on her one-inch heels. Wrung out, she leaned against the hallway wall. She had to accept the truth about Jack. He would do anything to protect the people he loved. Keep secrets, lie, even break the law. *Anything*. And because of that, she'd never be able to trust him.

A pain as sharp as a plunging dagger stabbed her chest and twisted in the cavity where her heart should be. Without trust, love couldn't survive.

"Hey Britt, can I have a word with you?"

Pivoting, she looked into the fresh face of Kyle Ayres. He was close to her age, but with his clear eyes and obvious enthusiasm for his new role as Grant's head counsel, he looked years younger than she felt right now.

A fresh tremor worked up her legs. She needed to sit down. She needed to absorb what Jack had done, what he'd forced her to do. She *didn't* need to begin sparring with Kyle. "Listen Kyle, I can't talk right now. We'll have to discuss Grant's case another time."

"How about later tonight?" He stared at her like

a child trying to cash in on a promised trip to Disneyland.

She'd agree to anything as long as he'd leave her alone. "Tonight? Yes, that's fine."

Kyle raised his wrist and glanced at his Rolex. The fluorescent lights glinted off diamond cufflinks. "It'll have to be late. I'm getting married tomorrow and my wedding rehearsal is tonight."

Britt nodded. She'd promised Jack she'd stay away from his family until after Kimberly's wedding to Kyle. Her head thrummed with emotion begging for release. "I'll be at the office all evening. When and where do you want to meet?"

He paused as if contemplating his busy schedule. "Say eleven o'clock at the Madison Club? That's right near your office."

Eleven o'clock. She exhaled with relief. She should be able to compose herself by then. "Fine. The Madison Club it is."

JACK LEANED against his patio railing and stared at the still water of Lake Mendota glistening in the moonlight. An ache throbbed at the center of his being. An ache so cold and deep he could barely draw breath. He was out on bail now, but he faced suspension, disbarment, and possibly a criminal trial. And the only damn thing he cared about was that Britt didn't believe him. She didn't trust him. And her lack of trust went far deeper than a fingerprint on the handle of a tapestry bag.

He tried to focus on the black water below, the water that had always brought him peace during tumultuous times in his past. This time the lake did nothing to comfort him. Nothing to reinstate his perspective. It only reminded him of Britt. Every damned thing reminded him of Britt.

The lobby buzzer sliced through his mind's morose wanderings. Wonderful. The last thing he needed was company.

He turned from the water, forcing his legs to carry him across the patio and toward the door. In the corner among a few stray autumn leaves, a black ribbon curled near the base of a barren planter. He stooped, picking up the wisp of ribbon. The ribbon he'd untied from Britt's hair the morning they'd made love. Staring at the black satin entwined in his fingers, the ache inside him grew intolerable.

The buzzer sounded again.

He shoved the ribbon into his pocket and entered his condo. He'd get rid of whoever was in the lobby and settle down with a bottle. If the lake couldn't wash these memories from his mind, maybe a fifth of whiskey could.

He crossed the living room and peered into the security monitor.

Kimberly peered back, concern obvious in her wide eyes and crinkle of brow.

Dismay seeped into his bones. He checked his watch. Tonight had been the rehearsal dinner for her wedding—a wedding in which both the best man and matron of honor were out on bail, pending trial. Kimberly had a lot to deal with, and yet she had stopped by after the event to support her big brother in his time of need.

His stomach clenched. He hated pity. Even from his sister, pity was unbearable. He'd spent his life making sure he was always on top. Making sure no one would ever have to pity him, protect him. My, how things had changed.

Punching the lock button, he buzzed her in and walked to the elevator to meet her. As soon as he'd reassured her that he was all right, he'd keep his date with that bottle. He could almost taste the sweet burn of the whiskey, almost feel the painful memories slip away.

The door swooshed open. Dressed to the nines in a sophisticated bride-to-be dress, Kimberly stood small and alone in the middle of the elevator. "Oh, Jackson," she moaned and rushed into his arms.

He wrapped his arms around her soft, delicate body. He'd rather face her pity than her anguish. He made a soothing hum deep in his throat. "It'll be all right, Kimberly. The truth will come out and everything will be all right." Apparently, he'd picked up some of Britt's confidence in the truth. At least he'd picked up the rhetoric.

She pulled out of his arms, shaking her head, tears welling in her doe eyes. "It will never be all right, Jackson. Grant is guilty. He murdered Tangi Rowe."

Disbelief shot through Jack like a red hot bullet. Grant guilty? Impossible. "Where the hell did you get that idea?"

Kimberly shrank from his bellow, clamping her jaw shut.

Kyle. That's who put that idea into her head. Jack toned his voice down. "Grant is not guilty, Kimberly. And Kyle shouldn't be discussing such things with you."

"He didn't want to tell me. I dragged it out of him."

Damn Kyle. No matter how Kimberly begged him,

he shouldn't have voiced his unfounded and false suspicions. Apparently, Jack needed to explain a few things to the little weasel. "Where is Kyle?"

"He has a meeting."

"A meeting? With whom?"

"Britt Gerritsen."

Jack clenched his teeth until his jaw ached. There was only one reason Kyle could have for meeting with Britt. "He's trying to cut a deal, isn't he? A plea bargain."

Tears overflowed and splashed onto Kimberly's freckled cheeks. Her body trembled with a restrained sob. "Kyle says Grant will spend less time in prison if he admits what he did. Kyle's trying to do what he thinks is best."

Best? Sending Grant to prison for a murder he didn't commit? Jack shook his head. It didn't make sense. Grant hadn't killed Tangi. Jack would stake his life on that fact.

He cupped his hand around his sister's cool cheek and forced patience into his voice. "Think about it, Kimberly. This is Grant we're talking about. Your brother. Do you believe Grant could murder someone?"

Tears flowed harder and her forehead knotted with turmoil. She shook her head as if trying to reconcile conflicting images. "But why would Kyle say he did?"

Good question. One he would love an answer to. He pivoted, staring through his darkened living room and out at the still, black water. How would Kyle benefit if Grant went to prison for murder? Was Kyle somehow involved in Tangi's death? Or could he be part of a cover-up?

''What are you thinking?''

Jack returned his gaze to his sister. All his life he'd tried to protect her from the ugliness of the world, the ugly undercurrents of the family. How on earth could he tell her he suspected her future husband may be part of this ugliness?

He reached in his pocket, fingering Britt's hair ribbon. Its satin softness curled around his fingers like a lover's embrace. Open, trusting, honest.

Like it or not, he had to tell Kimberly his suspicions. Whatever the cost, he had to allow her to make her own decisions about Kyle's motives. After all the mistakes Jack had made, he finally understood what Britt had known all along. Secrets didn't protect anyone, they led to heartache, to betrayal, to mistrust. ''No matter what he may believe about Grant, Kyle has no reason to enter a guilty plea at this time. I'm afraid he may have ulterior motives.''

Kimberly narrowed her eyes, confused. ''What do you mean?''

''Kyle may somehow be involved in Tangi's death. Or in the cover-up of her death.''

A cloud eclipsed Kimberly's innocent face. A cloud of disbelief. ''No.''

''Monday morning Judge Banks will decide whether the prosecution can introduce their evidence against Grant in court. If he decides they can't, the charges against Grant will be dropped. There's no reason for Grant to plead guilty before the judge makes his ruling. Kyle has to have a different reason for wanting Grant to plead. I think he might be trying to protect the real murderer.''

Kimberly's eyes darted around the room as if the truth was a physical enemy she was trying to escape.

The back of Jack's neck throbbed. His limbs filled with lead. He'd done it now. He'd broken his sister's heart. He'd destroyed the innocence he'd tried all her life to preserve.

Tears trickled down her face and dripped off her chin. "There must be some explanation. Kyle couldn't—"

Jack raised his hand to her face and wiped away her tears. "I don't know what's going on yet, Kimberly. But I have to find out. I have to stop this plea bargain. Where is Kyle meeting Britt?"

She brushed his hand away, staring into the air with shell-shocked eyes. The bright light of the entry hall's chandelier revealed the tightness around her mouth, the drawn quality of her cheeks. Suddenly, she looked far older than her twenty-two years. She looked weighed down with despair. "I overheard Daddy yelling at Grant one night about two months ago. Daddy knew Tangi was pregnant. He was angry that Grant would disgrace the family. I told Kyle every—" Her voice broke.

Compassion rocked Jack to his toes. He reached for his sister.

She shook her head and pushed his arms away. "Kyle promised me Daddy had nothing to worry about. He promised to make everything all right. And when he did, he said Daddy would be so grateful, he'd accept him like a real son."

Helplessness nagged at Jack's heart. His sister's world was crumbling, and he could do nothing to shield her from the pain. All he could do was listen.

She choked back a sob, her lower lip trembling. "The night Tangi was murdered, Kyle had car trouble. He had to have his car towed. He called me from a pay phone and asked me to pick him up.''

''You told the police. I read it in their reports.''

''I didn't tell them the pay phone was at a gas station two miles from where Tangi was found. I never thought it was important, until—''

Jack's heart doubled its pace. A possible picture of the events of that night took form in his mind. Kyle trying to convince Tangi to keep the affair and the baby secret. Kyle turning violent when she refused. Kyle driving a battered Tangi to the remote country highway. Kyle staging the car accident, hiking to town, and using Kimberly to establish his alibi. Kyle doing it all to curry favor with Roger.

Britt.

His heartbeat sputtered. Britt was meeting Kyle. Alone. Surely Kyle's request for a plea agreement would raise her suspicions just as it had raised Jack's. If she put two and two together…

He grabbed Kimberly's shoulders, forcing her to look at him. ''Where is Kyle, Kimberly? I have to stop that meeting.''

She met his gaze, her eyes still dazed. ''The Madison Club. You'd better hurry.''

He released his sister. With one glance back at her, he raced for the elevator. He had to reach Britt in time. If Kyle was involved in Tangi's death, he'd be desperate to keep it secret. So desperate he wouldn't hesitate to kill a suspicious assistant district attorney.

Chapter Fifteen

"Glad you could make it, Britt." Kyle Ayres stepped out of the shadow of the Madison Club's awning and thrust his hand toward her.

Britt jolted. She hadn't expected him until she got inside the club. She drew in a deep breath to calm her nerves and took his hand, giving it a firm shake. "Hello, Kyle. I thought we were meeting at the bar."

Lips crooking into a sheepish grin, he motioned over his shoulder at the entrance. "I was the only one inside. I didn't have the heart to make the bartender stick around just for me. How about we take a walk toward the Terrace?"

She turned in the direction of the Monona Terrace. The structure loomed like a cement monolith on the edge of Lake Monona. A dull light shone from the convention center entrance. No Lions' convention, no wedding reception this night. The long curving ramps leading to the roof terrace were quiet, empty. The Monona Terrace itself was as hushed as the silent, ice-rimmed lake. She shivered. The air was frigid, still. Its icy tendrils reached into her soul.

She forced herself to return Kyle's smile. By asking for this meeting, Kyle obviously wanted to find out what kind of a plea agreement she'd offer Grant if Judge Banks ruled in her favor. A good sign. A sign he didn't have as much faith in Grant's innocence as Jack did.

Jack. She pinched the bridge of her nose between thumb and forefinger. She couldn't think of Jack right now. She had to concentrate. If she could take advantage of Kyle's doubt and convince him to plead Grant *before* Judge Bank's ruling, she could keep her promise to Tangi.

Kyle led the way down the walk, the sound of his footsteps brittle in the crystal air.

She walked alongside him, shivering again. All night she'd been overly sensitive. Every sound made her jump. Every silence crept into her bones like an ominous truth. She stuffed her hands into the pockets of her trench coat and struggled to focus on Kyle.

"You're going to have to be gentle on me in this case, Britt. I've never defended anyone against murder charges before."

Britt nodded. If he expected gentle treatment, he was more inexperienced with murder trials than she'd dared hope.

"I'm used to dealing with balance sheets, not murder weapons and autopsy results. My talents lie in the business end of law. Or maybe politics. I've been considering running for public office. Do you think I could make it in politics?"

A movement near the doors leading into the convention center caught Britt's attention. A shadow. Her muscles tensed. She walked closer to Kyle's side. Ridiculous. She was imagining things. The shadow was a tree tossing in the wind.

Except there was no wind.

Kyle's voice cut through her paranoia. "I'm not interested in running for local office. I think I'd rather try for a national post. Maybe Grant's seat in the house. What do you think? Do I look like a congressman to you?"

She pulled her gaze from the Terrace and tuned in to his words. Since his promotion to Grant's head counsel this afternoon, the man's ambition had taken off like a runaway locomotive. "I think you'd better wait until Grant is behind bars before you try his title on for size. You're flirting with conflict of interest here, Kyle."

He threw his head back and chuckled, jets of steam rising in the cold air. "Conflict of interest? Really, Britt. After this afternoon's hearing, you shouldn't be pointing your finger at me."

She offered him an apologetic smile. She'd better get hold of herself. First she was imagining things, now she was jumping down Kyle's throat. She needed to gain his confidence, not insult him. The events of the past day—no, the past month—had eroded her poise. "You're right. Sorry, Kyle. It's been a tough day."

Touching her elbow, Kyle wrinkled his brow with exaggerated sympathy. "I understand."

A shiver slithered up Britt's spine and wrapped around her psyche. She could swear someone was watching her. She glanced over her shoulder. Nothing but the State Capitol's glowing dome and the hulking shadow of the City County Building. Kyle was right. She had to lighten up. "It's your meeting, Kyle. What do you want to discuss?"

Kyle's steps slowed and stopped. "What kind of a deal are you willing to offer?"

There it was, the opening she'd hoped for, out on the table. She fought to keep the smile from her lips. She couldn't seem too eager. She couldn't seem too desperate. It was time to put away her emotions and play the game of negotiation. "He's a murderer, Kyle. And with all the media focused on this case, the D.A.'s office can't appear to be too lenient."

"Listen, I was in Judge Banks' chambers for the hearing today. If it wasn't for Jack's arrest, the judge would have thrown out your evidence right then and there. I may not have a lot of experience with murder trials, but I do know that it's in your best interest to give me an attractive offer here."

Britt paused. Maybe she'd underestimated Kyle. Maybe his enthusiastic kid routine was an act. "I'll give you an attractive offer. Provided Grant pleads *before* Judge Banks rules on the shoes."

"That's a deal. What's your offer?"

Elation zinged along Britt's nerves like flame along a fast fuse. Wait one minute. The flame was extinguished by caution. He'd agreed too easily. "I'm not quite following you, Kyle."

Kyle raised his hands to his lips, forming a tent with his fingers. He seemed much older, more serious, not the silly kid dreaming about his career's bright future. "What's to follow? You make me a good offer, and Grant will plead before Judge Banks rules. Now what's your offer?"

Was she missing something here? Maybe she should take Kyle at his word. Maybe she shouldn't look a gift horse in the mouth, as they say. Unease crept up her spine, an anxiety she couldn't shake. "I still don't understand, Kyle. Why would you agree to my terms so easily?"

Kyle stopped and looked down at her as if he was explaining the ways of the world to a first-year law student. "The evidence shows Grant is guilty. Whether he gets off on a technicality or not, the public is always going to think of him as a murderer. And frankly, the family doesn't want the publicity."

"The family? You mean Roger."

"This deal is what Grant wants, too. He wants to pay for what he's done."

Not the Grant she knew. Either he had enjoyed a miraculous transformation, or Kyle was lying through his teeth.

"I wouldn't force my client into a plea bargain. I have nothing to gain if Grant goes to prison. Trust me."

Trust him? Britt didn't trust. Not anymore. Jack had taught her that lesson. And this time, she'd learned it well. "Before I offer anything, I'd like to talk to Grant."

Kyle's brow knotted and his eyes narrowed behind his stylish lenses. "Talk to Grant? Why? I'm giving you everything you want."

He was right. If Grant pled guilty, she'd insure he paid for his crime, she'd win favor with the district attorney, and most of all, she'd keep her promise to Tangi. Everything Kyle said was true.

But why was he saying it? "What is your interest in this, Kyle?"

He lowered his hands to his sides, his eyes wide and sincere. "My interest? I'm Grant's attorney, of course."

"As his attorney, you are obligated to do everything in your power to work for your client's best interest. How is it in Grant's best interest to plead guilty before Judge Banks decides on the evidence?''

He met her scrutiny, his eyes dead calm. ''It's what my client wants.''

''Then why isn't Grant here? Why can't I talk to him?''

Kyle stepped closer. Gone were the wide eyes. Gone was the sincerity. The lines of his face were hard and severe. ''I'll see to it that Grant confesses his crime to the court at his sentencing. That's all you have to concern yourself with. Now do your job. Give me an offer.''

Britt backed away from him. As much as she wanted to keep her promise to Tangi, as much as she wanted to make her best friend's murderer pay, she couldn't give Kyle an offer. Something wasn't right. She needed to find out what that something was. ''I won't make an offer until I talk to Grant.''

A grin spread across Kyle's lips. A grin lacking humor. ''All right. If you won't lower the charge, Grant will plead guilty to second-degree murder.''

What? Kyle had to be crazy to agree to propose a deal like this. No, not crazy. Desperate. But why would he want Grant to go to prison? Unless—Shock stuttered through her mind. Unless Kyle wasn't concerned with protecting Grant. Unless he was protecting someone else.

Alarm gripped her throat and coated her mouth, its flavor metallic and dry. Had she been wrong? Was Grant innocent of Tangi's murder? Had someone else killed her? Someone like Roger? After all, Kyle was nothing if not Roger's errand boy. She needed time to investigate before she agreed to *any* deal Kyle proposed. She forced a smile. "I'll talk to the D.A. and get back to you."

Kyle shook his head. "I want an answer now. This is your call. If you involve Fitzroy, he'll take you off the case. Then it will be too late."

"Too late for what, Kyle?"

"Justice."

"Justice?"

"Grant had the affair with Tangi. He got her pregnant. He's responsible for her death. *He's responsible.* You can't let him get away with murder the way he gets away with everything else." He grasped her arm, his fingers digging into her flesh.

Britt pulled back against his grip. "What are you doing? Let me go, Kyle."

"What's going on here?" a nasal voice broke the stillness. The shadows moved and Detective Cassidy emerged from the edge of the Monona Terrace and strode toward them.

She had never been so relieved to see someone—especially Cassidy. "I'm glad you're here, Detective. Mr. Ayres was getting a little out of hand."

Cassidy looked past her as if she were as insignificant as a buzzing mosquito. His beady gaze latched onto Kyle. Contempt twitched his lips. "Looks like I was right to keep an eye on you, Ayres."

Kyle dropped his hand from Britt's arm. "What are you doing here?"

Drawing a breath of frigid air, she summoned her most businesslike tone. "Detective, please escort Mr. Ayres to his car. This meeting is over."

Kyle waved his hand in the air as if brushing away her order. The dull glow of the streetlight glistened off the diamonds set in his cufflinks. "This meeting isn't over until we reach an agreement."

An agreement? After he'd manhandled her? He was dreaming. "Take my word for it, Kyle. The meeting is over. Detective?"

A low chuckle escaped Kyle's lips. "You think a crooked cop like Cassidy is going to help you? He takes his orders from Roger."

Britt snapped her head around to look at Cassidy. The incidents of his bungling cases and tainting evidence flashed through her mind. She'd always thought he was inept. Had he been crooked all along? "Detective? What do you say to this?"

"It's a bunch of garbage. Come with me, Kyle." Stepping in front of her, he grabbed Kyle's arm.

Kyle wrenched away. A sound like a muffled firecracker popped in the still air.

Cassidy's eyes widened. He slumped into Britt.

My God.

She tried to catch him, sticky warmth brushing her fingers. Unable to support his weight, she lowered Cassidy's body to the ground, alarm trembling along her arms to the tips of her fingers.

Kyle leaned over Cassidy, nudging his side with the toe of his shoe. A light caught the long silencer attached to the gun in Kyle's hand. *Kyle had shot Cassidy.*

And she was next. Fear breathed inside her like a living thing. She shoved Kyle. He sprawled across Cassidy's prone body. She whirled and ran in the only direction she could. Toward the Terrace.

Shouted obscenities defiled the air. Within seconds, Kyle's footsteps thundered behind her.

Her heels clattered on cement. Cold air rasped in

her throat. She ran in a weaving pattern so he couldn't get a clear shot. She needed help. She had to call the police. There were pay phones on the Terrace.

She dashed up the entrance ramp. The concrete wall next to her exploded, a shard of cement stinging her cheek. She kept running. Stride after stride. The cold air burned in her throat.

Reaching the top of the ramp, she ducked behind a long cement planter and crawled on her hands and knees across the cold cement. The pebbled concrete tiles ripped her knees and palms. She couldn't stop. She had to keep moving.

"Give it up, Britt." Kyle's voice echoed off the planters and cement tile. His footsteps halted. "There's no place to hide up here."

She crawled faster. Reaching the Otis Redding memorial, she ducked under the bench. She flattened her body to the ground, the cement achingly cold against her cheek.

Kyle stalked along the rail. The glow from a large globe light gleamed off the lenses of his glasses, the gun in his hand.

Her breath roared in her throat. Her heart struck a frantic tattoo in her chest. She tried to inhale quietly. She tried to hush the pounding of her heart. *Please, don't let him hear.*

"Britt, Britt, Britt." He walked in her direction. Each footfall splintered the still night like a gunshot. "Why couldn't you just do your job? Why couldn't you do your damn job?"

Adrenaline hummed in her ears. Her heart tumbled in her chest. Harder, faster, until she thought it might seize. She didn't dare move. She didn't dare breathe.

He walked closer. Past the concrete planter, past

the half wall overlooking the lake. Closer and closer to the bench she hid under. "Britt, Britt, Britt."

The soles of his shoes clicked on concrete. The same type of shoes Grant wore. The same type of shoes she'd found covered with mud, hidden in the tapestry bag.

Kyle. Kyle had killed Tangi. The realization hit her between the eyes with the force of a bullet. Kyle had killed Tangi and framed Grant.

He stopped, his pant leg brushing against the rough edge of the bench she hid under. "You had to screw everything up, didn't you Britt?"

A scream of rage welled in her throat. She choked it back, pressing her fingers hard against her lips. She couldn't give away her hiding place. She had to get to a phone. Once the police arrived, she could keep her promise to Tangi. Then she would make Kyle pay.

After what seemed like an eternity, he walked on. His footsteps grew faint. His mumbling faded away into the still night.

Britt dragged cold air into her lungs. She climbed to her knees. The vestibule was only a few yards away. She had to reach the phone and she had to do it quietly.

The night was cold and brittle as the thinnest skin of ice on water. No breeze in the leafless trees. No lapping of waves in the lake below. Nothing to mask even the slightest sound.

She had to make a break for it. And she had to do it now. She scrambled to her feet. Crouching low behind the long cement planter, she ran in the direction of the telephone. She struggled to keep her breathing hushed. To keep her heels from clicking on the concrete.

Reaching the vestibule, she paused. No footsteps. No whisper of air. No sound at all in the stillness around her. She grabbed the pay phone's receiver and raised her finger to the number pad.

A hand closed over her shoulder. A gun barrel pressed against her temple.

Oh, God.

The hand ripped the receiver from her grip and slammed it into place. Kyle whirled her around. The globe lights reflected off his glasses. The glare hid his eyes, leaving nothing but a blank, soulless stare.

Cold terror constricted her throat. Terror and rage. She clenched her hands into fists and forced her voice to function. "You killed Tangi, didn't you? But why?"

He shifted the gun, pressing the silencer against her cheek. "I just wanted to talk to her, convince her to keep her mouth shut. But she wouldn't listen. She was going to ruin the family." His face swam in a pool of light, a pool of shadows.

She closed her eyes for a moment, trying to steady herself. "Why frame Grant?"

"Grant doesn't deserve all he has. I'm the one Roger turns to. I'm the one who carries out his orders. I'm the one who acts like a real son. Grant does nothing, yet he gets everything. I only wanted to give him what he deserves. His irresponsibility killed Tangi Rowe. He deserves to pay."

"Britt?" A voice slashed the stillness. A voice deep and vibrant as life itself. Jack's voice. "Britt? Where the hell are you?"

She willed the clouds from her vision. Jack was

here. Jack was looking for her. A strangled sound tore from her lips.

"Shut the hell up." Kyle gripped her shoulder with excruciating force and whirled her around so her back pressed against his chest. Encircling her throat with his arm, he pressed the gun's silencer against her cheek. "I'm going down the ramp on the other side. And you're coming along. *Quietly.* If Jackson finds us, he's dead too."

A new fear scrambled up Britt's spine. A fear so potent and raw, it nearly jolted her to her knees. She couldn't let him kill Jack. Anything but that. "I'll do what you want."

She could almost feel Kyle's malevolent smile. "I thought so. Now move." He wrestled her away from the pay phone, almost slamming her head into the fire extinguisher hanging on the wall.

"Let her go, Kyle." Jack stepped out into the light. He approached slowly, suit jacket unbuttoned, hands held away from his sides like a gunfighter ready to draw. But she could see no weapon. Nothing but a wisp of black in one clenched fist. Jack was unarmed.

Britt's stomach lurched. Jack had heard her and rushed to protect her. And that instinct, that wonderful protective instinct was going to get him killed.

"Don't come any closer, Jackson," Kyle barked. "One more step and she's dead."

The muscle in Jack's jaw clenched, his face hard as stone. His gaze flicked to Britt and back to Kyle. "Like you killed Tangi, Kyle? Like you shot Detective Cassidy?"

"Not one more step." His diamond cufflink dug into Britt's throat. His breathing quickened, steam rising over her shoulder and into the still air.

Not five feet away, Jack stopped. "Cassidy's not dead, Kyle. He's still quite alive, and an ambulance should be here for him any minute."

Kyle scoffed in Britt's ear. "I don't hear any sirens. It had to take you a couple of minutes to get up here and find us. And if you called for an ambulance or the cops, they would be here already."

Jack's expression remained hard, unreadable. "Kimberly knows, Kyle."

"You're lying."

"How do you think I knew you and Britt were meeting tonight? How do you think I knew where to find you? Kimberly put the pieces together. She knows you killed Tangi. She knows you tried to frame Grant."

Kyle lowered the gun ever so slightly, shaking his head. "Even if she knows, Kimberly would never give me up. She'd never go to the police. You're out of luck."

For the briefest of seconds, Jack's gaze met Britt's. He looked at the wall of the vestibule and then back to her before again focusing on Kyle.

She glanced at the wall out of the corner of her eye. The fire alarm. Jack had looked at the fire alarm next to the pay phone.

"What about Roger? When I left Kimberly, she was headed to the house. You don't think she'd keep something as important as you framing Grant secret from our father, do you?"

Kyle shifted his feet, the soles of his shoes scraping against pebbled cement. "You're bluffing. Kimberly isn't going to tell anybody."

Jack's dark eyes once again flicked to the fire alarm and back to Britt. For a moment he held her gaze.

"Trust me," he said, then his focus returned to Kyle. "Kimberly doesn't keep anything from our father. He wouldn't allow it. You can trust me on that."

Trust me. Jack's words echoed in Britt's ears. Words he had meant for her, not for Kyle. Without moving her head, she glanced at the fire alarm. The lever was two steps away. Two steps and she could call for help.

But what would Kyle do if she took those two steps? He'd shoot her. Shoot Jack.

Trust me. She clenched her fists, her palms clammy and cold. Could she trust Jack?

Under her scrutiny, the planes of his face seemed to soften. A spark of idealism, of love, burned deep in his dark eyes. No, more than a spark. A blazing fire.

A fire that warmed her soul.

Looking into his eyes, she believed in him. God help her, she *believed*. A belief beyond evidence. Beyond fingerprints. Beyond secrets. A belief beyond logic and reason itself.

Of course she could trust him. He would protect her for the same reason he'd always protected her. Love. Pure and simple.

Jack raised his hand, the wisp of black she'd noticed earlier clutched in his fingers.

"Don't move, Jackson," Kyle bellowed, his voice vibrating with anger. He pressed the silencer harder against her cheek. "I'm warning you, I'll kill her. Whatever you have in your hand, drop it."

Britt forced herself to remain still, remain calm. Whatever Jack was up to, she'd play her part and trust him to do the rest.

Hand still raised, Jack stepped forward. One step. Two steps.

Kyle reared back, releasing her throat. Swinging his gun around, he aimed at Jack's chest.

Now.

Britt lunged for the fire alarm. A muffled pop exploded in the silent air. A gunshot.

She yanked the lever. A deafening blare fractured the quiet like a frantic scream.

Kyle pointed the gun at her forehead.

In that split second, Jack plowed into his middle with the force of a linebacker.

Kyle staggered backwards, slamming into the wall.

Jack lurched and stumbled toward him as if in slow motion. A black glossy stain spread down his thigh. The stain of blood.

Jack had been shot.

No! Please, no!

Jack struck Kyle's arm. A flash of metal skittered across the rough cement. The gun. Back against the wall, Kyle punched back, slamming his fists into Jack's face.

She had to do something. She had to stop Kyle. She grabbed the extinguisher from the wall next to her. Clutching the heavy canister with clammy hands, she hefted it into the air. And brought it down on Kyle's skull.

He crumpled to the ground, his glasses shattering on the cement.

Sirens rose above the throb of the fire alarm.

Britt knelt by Jack's side. Her vision narrowed until she could see only him.

Eyes closed, Jack slumped against the wall. Blood spread out in a dark pool around his leg, a pool ever widening, ever growing. A black satin ribbon lay crumpled in his palm. Her hair ribbon.

She brushed a lock of dark hair from his forehead, his skin warm under her fingertips. "Jack. Please. Can you hear me?"

He didn't stir.

Ripping off her trench coat, she pressed it against his thigh to stifle the flow of blood. "I'm sorry I didn't believe you. I'm sorry I had you arrested. Oh, God, I love you, Jack."

His face was so battered. So pale. Drained of all color. Drained of all life.

He couldn't die. She wouldn't let him. "Damn you, Jack. I trusted you to get us both out of this alive, not just me. You can't let me down."

He opened a dark eye. "Britt," he murmured through gritted teeth. "I'd never dream of letting you down."

Chapter Sixteen

Dodging carts of breakfast trays, Britt hurried down the corridor leading to Jack's hospital room. She glanced at the room numbers flanking each door, quickening her steps when she spotted Jack's. When she'd left his room to make her phone calls, he'd been groggy, slipping in and out of consciousness. Certainly in no shape to talk. A tremor danced along her nerves. Would he be fully awake now?

She pushed open the door and focused on the bed.

Nothing but rumpled sheets stared back.

Where was he?

A sound came from behind the open door. A rustle, then a mumbled curse.

"Jack?"

Breath whistled through tight lips. "Britt. Thank God. Come on in. Shut the door behind you."

Pulse quickening at the low rumble of his voice, she did as he asked.

Behind the door, Jack balanced on his left leg, crutches canted under his arms like the guide wires of a radio tower. Naked except for briefs, he struggled to pull a pair of sweatpants over his bandaged right leg. The sheen of perspiration covered his chest like baby oil on a body builder, transforming his awkward task into a symphony of flexing muscle and taut sinew.

Tenderness gripped her heart. "Hold on, I'll help you."

"Thanks. I never thought getting dressed could be so damn hard." He gritted his teeth with obvious pain.

She knelt beside him and stretched the soft fleece over his bandage. "When I stepped out, you weren't awake. Has the doctor released you already?"

"I'm releasing myself."

"And you think that's a good idea?"

"If the doctor wants me to stay in bed, he'll have to tie me down. I don't have time to waste in a damn hospital bed. I was coming to find you."

A warm jitter worked its way through every cell of her body. Funny. As a girl when she'd dreamed of being in love, she'd always imagined a calm security like a favorite fluffy blanket. Maybe that tranquility would come later. Judging from the slamming pressure of her pulse, she was anything but tranquil now. "Looks like I got here just in time. Now why don't you sit down on the bed and I'll tell you what I've been up to."

He remained rooted to his spot. "I already know what you've been up to."

"Oh?"

"You conferred with the D.A., and you're dropping all charges against Grant and me."

She didn't even try to hide her surprise. "How do you know?"

"Roger."

Roger. She had to tell him about Roger. Despite all

the bad feelings between them, Jack was still Roger's son. Her news would hurt him. And the last thing she wanted to do was hurt him. "Cassidy spilled his guts, Jack. It seems that since Gianni's conviction, Cassidy has been on Roger's payroll. The police are launching a full-blown investigation."

Jack nodded, his attempt at a smile fading. "Believe me, he's preparing himself for the war. You'll have your hands full."

"There's more. According to Cassidy, Roger paid him to report Tangi's death was nothing more than an accident and to cover up evidence of murder. He was afraid Grant would become a suspect. If my dad hadn't been listening to his police scanner, I might have never known she was murdered."

"But he was. And you did."

She nodded. And with Kyle behind bars, she was on her way to keeping her promise to Tangi.

Jack brushed a strand of hair off her forehead. "Those aren't the reasons I wanted to see you."

A little wave of anticipation rippled over her. "Jack, I thought—"

He touched a finger to her lips, silencing her with the lightest of contact. "You have to listen to me. Last night, I never got a chance to tell you." He withdrew his touch, brow knotting, obviously struggling to come up with the right words.

Britt drew in a long stabilizing breath. The caress of his fingertip against her lips lingered like a sweet dream.

"Britt, I just want—I have to—Oh, hell. I've been such a damn idiot. A damn idiot. But I've learned my lesson. I know I can't protect you from the truth. I don't even want a woman who needs that kind of protection. I want a true partner, Britt.''

Blinding moisture stung her eyes. She blinked back the tears. He'd just given her everything she'd waited for, longed for. ''I—''

He held up a hand. ''Don't say anything yet. First, I want to clear everything up. I don't want anything between us. Not the slightest sliver of doubt.''

She couldn't help but smile. ''After last night, how could I doubt you?''

''I want to make sure you still don't think I hid the muddy shoes in my study to protect Grant.''

She swallowed the sweet lump in her throat. ''I trust you, Jack.''

''But I've hidden the truth before to protect someone I love. I just want to make sure you know it's different this time.''

Memories stirred in that vulnerable place she'd hidden away inside her. Their engagement party, Roger's threats, her father's secret. It was all so long ago. A distant echo. Another life. Everything *was* different now. So different.

''I touched the handle of Tia's bag, but I didn't know what was in it. Tia finally admitted she threw the bag and shoes away in her misguided attempt to protect Grant. Kyle must have seen her and used Kimberly's key to plant the bag in my study.'' He looked deep into her eyes. ''I didn't hide the shoes, Britt.''

''I know. You didn't have a reason to hide them. You never believed Grant was guilty. And you certainly wouldn't hide evidence that might lead to the real killer. I said I trust you, Jack, and I mean it.''

Leaning on his crutches, he took her hands in his. ''There will be times in the future, rough times, and we'll have to get through them together. I want you to know you can always count on me. I want you to know that I'll always tell you the truth. I want you to marry me, Britt.''

Her heart seemed to swell until she feared it would burst. "I love you. Everything about you. I love the way you follow through on your dreams. The way you look out for your mom and sister. Your dry sense of humor and the way that lock of hair hangs over your forehead when you're asleep.''

She swallowed a giggle. "Even your sarcasm. I even love your sarcasm and the way you like to play the underdog fighting the big bad government.''

His gaze claimed her, dark and fathomless as the pain that had once plagued her heart. The pain that was fast becoming a faded memory.

"I love all of you, Jack. Your virtues, your faults, all of you.''

A chuckle rose from his lips, contagious, full of the energy of life, of love. "My faults? What faults?''

She couldn't help but smile. "I'll marry you. I'd love to marry you.''

Peering at her out of the corner of his eye, he frowned. "One more thing. I hate to disappoint you, but I don't think we should have an engagement party this time. Just to be safe.''

She shook her head. The man was impossible. Incorrigible. Insufferable. And she didn't want to live one more day without him. "Don't worry. This time we'll elope. Do you think we could find someone to marry us at that ranch of yours? In the valley where you first proposed?''

"I don't know why not.'' A mischievous grin

stretched across his lips and glowed in his eyes. "And after we elope, what then?"

Her mind whirled with possibilities. "Then I'm going to lock you in the bedroom and I'm not going to let you out until I have a baby in my arms."

He let the crutches clatter to the floor and reached for her, pulling her into his strong, warm embrace. "Only one?"

She snuggled against his chest and raised her lips to meet his. His kiss sent fire racing through her veins and love spinning through her mind in giddy pinwheels of color. No, one child wouldn't be enough. Not nearly enough.

Damn Jack. He was right again.

Outside, it looks like a
charming old building
near the Baltimore
waterfront, but inside
lurks danger...
and romance.

**"First lady of suspense"
Ruth Glick** writing as
Rebecca York returns with

#582 AMANDA'S CHILD
On Sale September 2000

Pregnant virgin Amanda Barnwell never imagined
that a trip to the sperm bank would make her
the target of two very powerful and dangerous
families. Amanda found protection and more in
the arms of Matt Forester. But was love enough to
see them through to happily-ever-after?

Available at your favorite retail outlet.

Visit us at www.eHarlequin.com   HI43L2

If you enjoyed what you just read,
then we've got an offer you can't resist!

Take 2 bestselling love stories FREE!

Plus get a FREE surprise gift!

Clip this page and mail it to Harlequin Reader Service®

IN U.S.A.	IN CANADA
3010 Walden Ave.	P.O. Box 609
P.O. Box 1867	Fort Erie, Ontario
Buffalo, N.Y. 14240-1867	L2A 5X3

YES! Please send me 2 free Harlequin Intrigue® novels and my free surprise gift. Then send me 4 brand-new novels every month, which I will receive before they're available in stores. In the U.S.A., bill me at the bargain price of $3.57 plus 25¢ delivery per book and applicable sales tax, if any*. In Canada, bill me at the bargain price of $3.96 plus 25¢ delivery per book and applicable taxes**. That's the complete price and a savings of at least 10% off the cover prices— what a great deal! I understand that accepting the 2 free books and gift places me under no obligation ever to buy any books. I can always return a shipment and cancel at any time. Even if I never buy another book from Harlequin, the 2 free books and gift are mine to keep forever. So why not take us up on our invitation. You'll be glad you did!

181 HEN C22Y
381 HEN C22Z

Name	(PLEASE PRINT)	
Address	Apt.#	
City	State/Prov.	Zip/Postal Code

THE SECRET IS OUT!

HARLEQUIN®

I N T R I G U E ®

presents

By day these agents are cowboys;
by night they are specialized
government operatives.
Men bound by love, loyalty and the law—
they've vowed to keep their missions
and identities confidential....

Harlequin Intrigue

Harlequin American Romance
(a special tie-in story)

HARLEQUIN®
Makes any time special ™

Visit us at www.eHarlequin.com   HITC

HARLEQUIN
Duets™

*Pick up a Harlequin Duets™
from August–October 2000
and receive $1.00 off the
original cover price.* *

*Experience the "lighter side of love"
in a Harlequin Duets™.
This unbeatable value just became
irresistible with our special introductory
price of $4.99 U.S./$5.99 CAN. for
2 Brand-New, Full-Length
Romantic Comedies.*

Visit us at www.eHarlequin.com   HDMKD

HARLEQUIN®

I N T R I G U E®

COMING NEXT MONTH

#581 THE BODYGUARD'S ASSIGNMENT by Amanda Stevens
Texas Confidential

Agent Brady Morgan's specialty was witness protection, and Grace Drummond was his downfall. The crime she had witnessed incriminated a dangerous criminal, placing her in serious danger. And the secret Grace kept was one that Brady needed to uncover if he intended to keep them safe and rebuild the love they'd once shared.

#582 AMANDA'S CHILD by Ruth Glick writing as Rebecca York
43 Light Street

When a sperm bank pregnancy endangered virgin Amanda Barnwell's life, Matt Forester appointed himself as her guardian. Caught between two powerful families, Amanda needed Matt's name to protect her unborn child and provide her safety. Only by exposing the true source of the threats could they begin a new life—together.

#583 SAFE BY HIS SIDE by Debra Webb
Secret Identity

"Kate Roberts" didn't remember who she was or how she'd found special-agent-in-hiding Jack Raine—but now, a killer was after them both. And though her returning memories hinted she might have been used to betray Jack, she knew there was nowhere she'd be safer than by his side....

#584 UNDERCOVER PROTECTOR by Cassie Miles

Officer Annie Callahan returned home to simplify her life and instead found herself faced with Michael Slade—a man she'd once loved deeply. Now working undercover, Michael knew Annie was in danger from a stalker and possibly more. Revealing his identity was not an option, so he became her fiancé. Could Michael keep Annie safe—and perhaps get her to fall in love with him all over again?

Visit us at www.eHarlequin.com